This Scheming
World

Ihara Saikaku

This Scheming World

Classic Tales of Desire, Deception
and Greed in Old Japan

Translated by
Masanori Takatsuka and David C. Stubbs

Revised and with a New Introduction by
David J. Gundry

TUTTLE Publishing
Tokyo | Rutland, Vermont | Singapore

"Books to Span the East and West"

Tuttle Publishing was founded in 1832 in the small New England town of Rutland, Vermont [USA]. Our core values remain as strong today as they were then—to publish best-in-class books which bring people together one page at a time. In 1948, we established a publishing outpost in Japan—and Tuttle is now a leader in publishing English-language books about the arts, languages and cultures of Asia. The world has become a much smaller place today and Asia's economic and cultural influence has grown. Yet the need for meaningful dialogue and information about this diverse region has never been greater. Over the past seven decades, Tuttle has published thousands of books on subjects ranging from martial arts and paper crafts to language learning and literature—and our talented authors, illustrators, designers and photographers have won many prestigious awards. We welcome you to explore the wealth of information available on Asia at **www.tuttlepublishing.com**.

Published by Tuttle Publishing, an imprint of Periplus Editions (HK) Ltd.

www.tuttlepublishing.com

Copyright © 2023 Periplus Editions (HK) Ltd.

Library of Congress Cataloging-in-Publication Data is in progress

ISBN: 978-4-8053-1710-5

26 25 24 23
10 9 8 7 6 5 4 3 2 1   2307CM

Printed in China

TUTTLE PUBLISHING® is a registered trademark of Tuttle Publishing, a division of Periplus Editions (HK) Ltd.

Distributed by

North America, Latin America & Europe
Tuttle Publishing
364 Innovation Drive
North Clarendon
VT 05759-9436 U.S.A.
Tel: 1 (802) 773-8930
Fax: 1 (802) 773-6993
info@tuttlepublishing.com
www.tuttlepublishing.com

Japan
Tuttle Publishing
Yaekari Building 3rd Floor
5-4-12 Osaki Shinagawa-ku,
Tokyo 141 0032
Tel: (81) 3 5437-0171
Fax: (81) 3 5437-0755
sales@tuttle.co.jp
www.tuttle.co.jp

Asia Pacific
Berkeley Books Pte. Ltd.
3 Kallang Sector #04-01
Singapore 349278
Tel: (65) 6741-2178
Fax: (65) 6741-2179
inquiries@periplus.com.sg
www.tuttlepublishing.com

Contents

Introduction

Ihara Saikaku and His Fiction

The stories and novels[1] of Ihara Saikaku[2] (1642–1693), widely acknowledged as the most accomplished Japanese writer of fiction during the first half of the Tokugawa period[3] (1600–1867), portray the lives of characters from the officially designated status-groups that together comprised the bulk of Japanese society: samurai, *chōnin* (urban commoners)[4] and peasants. Although Saikaku wrote many sa-

---

[1] There is much debate surrounding the questions of what constitutes a novel and whether works properly designated by this term were produced in Japan prior to the digestion of Western novels by Japanese writers starting in the late 19th century. Here, for simplicity's sake, I use the term in its broadest sense: a long work of prose fiction.

[2] The pen name of Hirayama Tōgo.

[3] Also known as the Edo period after the location of the Tokugawa shoguns' seat of government.

[4] *Chōnin* were in principle divided into craftsmen and merchants, but this appears to have been more a matter of Confucian theory rather than legal practice (David J. Gundry, *Parody, Irony and Ideology in the Fiction of Ihara Saikaku* [Leiden: Brill, 2017], p. 201; David L. Howell, *Geographies of*

murai-focused narratives, in the popular imagination in today's Japan he is best known for his depictions of *chōnin* life,
perhaps because he himself was a wealthy *chōnin* and because
complex portrayals of people engaged in commerce were new
in Saikaku's day, whereas Japanese bards and writers had been
producing literary portrayals of samurai exploits for hundreds
of years.

This Scheming World (1693)[5] provides perhaps the most
striking example of this refreshingly modern focus on the economic activities of businesspeople at all levels of 17th-century
Japan's burgeoning bourgeoisie. Like other collections of tales
by Saikaku, its otherwise diverse stories are connected by a
shared theme, in this case the efforts of debtors to pay off
their debts as they come due on New Year's Eve, or, absent the
funds to do so, to avoid or fend off bill collectors, as well as
the strategies used by these to extract money from them. The
stories include much detail regarding material culture, interest
rates, the prices of commodities and consumer goods, as well
as portrayals of the pursuit of the sort of costly pleasures that
land their characters in debt, such as theatrical performances
and the services of female and male prostitutes. What emerges
is a remarkably full and vibrant portrait of cities and towns
whose inhabitants of every social level are linked by business
transactions.

A comparison of Saikaku's fiction with that of his great
aristocratic predecessor Murasaki Shikibu (c. 973–c. 1014)

Identity in Nineteenth-Century Japan [Berkeley: University of California
Press, 2005], pp. 24–25; Mark Metzler, Gregory Smits, "Introduction:
The Autonomy of Market Activity and the Emergence of *Keizai*
Thought," in Bettina Gramlich-Oka, Gregory Smits, eds., *Economic
Thought in Early Modern Japan* [Leiden: Brill, 2010], pp. 6–7).
[5] Japanese title *Seken mune san'yō*.

tells us much of what is distinctive about both and sheds light on key aspects of premodern Japan's cultural and social history. *The Tale of Genji* (early 1000s), Murasaki Shikibu's sprawling novel of erotic intrigue in the imperial court, features complex descriptions of characters' motivations and states of mind that have no equivalent in Western fiction until the emergence of the modern psychological novel centuries later. Saikaku's fiction lacks *Genji's* psychological complexity but gives a much broader overview of society. Writing after the development of printing in nearby China but centuries before the emergence of a publishing industry in Japan and, apparently, of a literate middle class to support one, Murasaki Shikibu wrote about and for the tiny Japanese aristocracy of her time; her magnum opus was copied by hand and circulated on a non-commercial basis among the members of her class. Commercial publishing finally got a foothold in Japan around the beginning of the Tokugawa period.[6] Saikaku's books were published and sold by this industry during its first century and appear to have been bestsellers. *Genji's* title character, the emperor's favorite son, is portrayed as so out of touch with the lives of ordinary people that he does not recognize the sound of rice being polished with a treadle mortar,[7] and its important characters are all members of the aristocracy. The characters in Saikaku's fiction range from high-ranking samurai to impoverished peasants and cut-rate streetwalkers, and his stories include so much information about the nuts-and-bolts of characters' workaday lives that when searching Japanese dictionaries for

---

[6] Peter Kornicki, *The Book in Japan: A Cultural History from the Beginnings to the Nineteenth Century* (Honolulu: University of Hawai'i Press, 2001), pp. 173–75.

[7] Murasaki Shikibu, trans. Royall Tyler, *The Tale of Genji* (New York: Penguin, 2003), p. 63.

the names of now obsolete items encountered in these texts, one is likely to find the very sentences one is reading given as examples of their usage.

After establishing himself as a virtuoso composer of *haikai* linked verse, which copied the forms of Japanese court poetry while deliberately violating its strict rules of diction and decorum, Saikaku added fiction to his repertoire, writing *The Life of an Amorous Man* (1682),[8] a comic novel that presents its voluptuary protagonist Yonosuke as a contemporary, wealthy *chōnin* counterpart to both the title character of *Genji* and Ariwara no Narihira (825–880), the historical but heavily mythologized presumed romantic hero of *Genji*'s literary predecessor *Tales of Ise* (900s). *Amorous Man*'s densely allusive style, which incorporates many references to these works as well as to nō dramas and Japanese and Chinese poetry, shows the influence of Saikaku's background in the similarly allusive *haikai* genre and transfers the prestige of Heian-period court aristocrats and other elites of the past to the milieu of wealthy Tokugawa-period commoners.[9]

Published eleven years after *Amorous Man*, *This Scheming World* features fewer such allusions, a change that one might attribute to the waning influence of *haikai* on Saikaku's fiction or a greater confidence, born of the commercial success of his tales of *chōnin* life, in the ability of such narratives to attract readers' interest without constantly invoking real or fictional culture heroes of times past.[10]

---

[8] Japanese title *Kōshoku ichidai otoko*.

[9] Gundry, *Parody, Irony and Ideology*, p. 82.

[10] David J. Gundry, "Hierarchy, Hubris, and Parody in Ihara Saikaku's *Kōshoku ichidai otoko*," *The Journal of Japanese Studies*, Vol. 43, No. 2, Summer 2017, pp. 386–87; Gundry, *Parody, Irony and Ideology*, pp. 73–74; Maeda Kingorō, *Kinsei bungaku zakkō* (Tokyo: Bensei Shuppan,

A collection of stories about indebtedness of course lends itself to the inclusion of moral lessons, which are indeed to be found in *This Scheming World*. However, as Jeffrey Johnson has pointed out, Saikaku's narratives frequently undermine their own moralizing,[11] and this holds true for *This Scheming World*. In one passage the collection extols extreme frugality and in another lampoons it or waxes poetic about all the wonderful things money can buy. In the opening paragraph of "The One-*Monme* Society" the narrator denies that luck is a factor in the acquisition of wealth, whereas the narrator of "The Pillar Rice-Cakes of Nagasaki" refers to good luck as "the *sine qua non* of riches." Perhaps the most striking example of this sort of seemingly playful equivocation is to be found in the story "Sensible Advice on Domestic Economy," in which a long list of the advantages to be gained by a head of household when he stays home (i.e., away from brothels) in the evenings is followed by a similarly lengthy passage describing the wives of men of various social levels as pale imitations of the various levels of prostitute. The passage concludes with the observation that wives, in contrast to prostitutes, are disappointing "in any and all respects." One could easily interpret such contrasting assertions as an ironic engagement with the tradition of Confucian morality tales produced in both China and Japan, and as subtle pushback against the self-censorship necessary to keep from provoking Tokugawa authorities wary of the potential of popular culture to morally corrupt those who consumed it, or even

---

2006), p. 225; Taniwaki Masachika, *Saikaku kenkyū josetsu* (Tokyo: Shintensha, 1981), pp. 151–76.

[11] Jeffrey Johnson, "Saikaku and the Narrative Turnabout," *The Journal of Japanese Studies*, Vol. 27, No. 2 (2001), pp. 336, 341. See also Howard Hibbett, *The Floating World in Japanese Fiction* (New York: Oxford University Press, 1959), pp. 3, 18, 19–22.

as a reflection of Mahayana Buddhism's doctrine of nonduality, which teaches that distinctions between phenomena are illusory, and of its resultant undermining of cut-and-dried rules.

Sexuality and Prostitution in Tokugawa Japan

The many varieties of prostitution in the Japan of Saikaku's day play a major role in his fiction. At the top of the hierarchy of female prostitutes were those working in the licensed prostitution quarters of major cities and various towns. These women were divided into ranks, with regulated prices for the services of those at each level. Licensed prostitutes of the higher ranks were supposed to be accomplished in the arts and capable of sophisticated conversation, which is reflected in the characterization of prostitutes as models imperfectly emulated by married women, cited above. There were various forms of unlicensed prostitution as well, such as teahouses providing sexual services, which feature in the stories collected here.

Male prostitution, in particular that involving kabuki actors, was also an integral feature of urban life, and plays a significant though not major part in *This Scheming World*. Both Saikaku's fiction and other texts from the period imply a sort of normative bisexuality among males. The social conventions governing sexual interactions between males were age-structured, and relationships conforming to these involved an adult male and an adolescent boy, with the senior partner acting as the pursuer and penetrator of the junior. The passage from youth into adulthood was marked by the rite of *genbuku*, which involved the donning of adult clothes and a change in hairstyle, such that the distinction between men and youths, the latter being legitimate objects of erotic pursuit by the former, was clearly visually coded. Adolescent boys had corners

shaven into their hairlines just above the temples, and the
crowns of their heads were shaven as well, but a youth's forelocks were left unshaven until his *genbuku*, which in Saikaku's
fiction tends to be performed around the age of eighteen. If a
youth was romantically involved with an adult male, once the
youth's forelocks were shaven the sexual aspect of their rela-
tionship was supposed to end, but Saikaku's fiction character-
izes the emotional bond between the former lovers as
outlasting those between men and women.[12]

In texts from medieval and early modern Japan sexual relationships between males are depicted as most closely associ-
ated with the samurai, Buddhist monasticism and the
prostitution of kabuki actors.[13] This is reflected in the contents of Saikaku's one volume of fiction exclusively focused on
sex and romance between males, *The Great Mirror of Male
Love* (1687), which is divided into a section featuring tales of
same-sex love among samurai males and another focused on
the prostitution of kabuki actors, who, like female prostitutes
in other works of fiction by Saikaku, are often depicted as be-
coming romantically involved with a particular customer. The
fact that when the stories in *This Scheming World* allude to this
variety of sex and romance it is in the context of kabuki prostitution reflects the fact that their principal characters are

---

[12] Gundry, *Parody, Irony and Ideology*, pp. 85, 91, 96, 98–99, 123 note 13.

[13] For a fuller treatment of age-structured male homosexuality in medieval
and early-modern Japan, see Gundry, *Parody, Irony and Ideology*, pp. 37–
39; Gary P. Leupp, *Male Colors: The Construction of Homosexuality in
Tokugawa Japan* (Berkeley: University of California Press, 1995); Gregory M. Pflugfelder, *Cartographies of Desire: Male-Male Sexuality in Japanese Discourse*, 1600–1950 (Berkeley: University of California Press,
1999), pp. 1–145, 235–85; Paul Gordon Schalow, Introduction, in Ihara
Saikaku, trans. Paul Gordon Schalow, *The Great Mirror of Male Love*
(Stanford: Stanford University Press, 1990).

chōnin, not samurai.

Although such relationships between males were tolerated and even celebrated in Japanese culture at a time when both homo- and heterosexual anal sex, as the crime of sodomy, were a capital offense throughout Western Europe, it would be mistaken to conclude from this fact that Japan was an island of sexual liberalism and license in the seventeenth century. Adultery, defined as sex between a married woman and any man other than her husband, was punishable by death, as depicted in the second and third novellas of Saikaku's *Five Women Who Loved Love*.[14] (This is not the case in the Heian-period aristocratic world portrayed in *Genji*.) Heads of household appear to have had de facto sexual access to servants working there, who were not free to leave during a contract period, and samurai heads of household in Saikaku's fiction are shown as exercising their power of life and death over household members when a maidservant or pageboy sharing the master's bed is discovered to have had sex with someone else, or mistakenly thought to have done so.[15]

Licensed quarter prostitutes and prostituted kabuki actors typically became indentured through contracts that obliged them to spend years working off the signing bonus pocketed by their families, who, in a drastic move to get out of financial difficulty, essentially sold their offspring, sometimes in very early adolescence, to those who would pimp them. Saikaku's fiction occasionally acknowledges the suffering caused by this system without going so far as to suggest that reform was in order.

---

[14] Ihara Saikaku, trans. Wm. Theodore de Bary, *Five Women Who Loved Love* (Rutland: Tuttle, 1956), pp. 73–156.

[15] Gundry, *Parody, Irony and Ideology*, pp. 219–24; Ihara, Schalow, *Great Mirror of Male Love*, 2:2, pp. 97–104.

14

The Historical Context

This is unsurprising given that any content that could be interpreted as critical of the Tokugawa regime risked incurring the displeasure of the authorities. One could take the praising references to Tokugawa rule in the preface to *This Scheming World* and in both the preface of *Exemplary Tales of the Way of the Warrior*[16] (1687) and the opening of its first story[17] as an attempt to offset implications in the stories that follow that not all is well in Tokugawa Japan. This is not to say that this praise was necessarily insincere; the Tokugawa had put an end to nearly a century and a half of civil war and had presided over rapid economic growth that had brought unprecedented prosperity to Japan.[18]

The preface to *This Scheming World* was omitted from the original 1965 edition of this translation; I have translated it for inclusion in the revised edition both in order to present readers with all of Saikaku's book and because the preface's reference to the Tokugawa peace is an important indicator of its historical context, which I shall further elucidate to help set the scene of its stories.

Except for a brief period during the 1300s in which Emperor Godaigo (1288–1339) attempted to regain de facto power, from the late 1100s until the Meiji Restoration in 1868, the emperor filled the role of symbolic head of state, whereas a hereditary military dictator usually referred to in English as the shogun functioned as the de facto head of state. During

---

[16] Japanese title *Budō denraiki*.

[17] Gundry, *Parody, Irony and Ideology*, p. 197; Ihara Saikaku, *Budō denraiki*, in Fuji Akio, Hiroshima Susumu, eds., *Shinpen Nihon koten bungaku zenshū*, Vol. 69: *Ihara Saikaku shū 4* (Tokyō: Shōgakukan, 2000), pp. 17, 21.

[18] Gundry, *Parody, Irony and Ideology*, p. 262.

Japan's Sengoku ("Warring States") period, which began with Ōnin War in 1467, the country was divided into squabbling fiefdoms that kept the country in a state of intermittent civil war. The three warlords known as "the Great Unifiers," Oda Nobunaga (1534–1582), Toyotomi Hideyoshi (1536–1598) and Tokugawa Ieyasu (1542–1616) each brought increasing amounts of territory under centralized control, culminating in Ieyasu's unification of the country after his and his allies' forces' victory at the Battle of Sekigahara in 1600. Ieyasu founded the Tokugawa shogunal dynasty and set up its de facto capital in Edo (now known as Tokyo), whereas the emperor continued to serve as the symbolic head of state in Kyoto, where the imperial capital had been established in 794. Most samurai were compelled to live in provincial capitals under the supervision and in the pay of the lord of each province, known as a daimyo. Daimyo were required to spend every other year in attendance at the shogun's court in Edo, where they had to leave their wives and children, in effect as hostages of the shogunate, in order to ensure that daimyo would not start rebellions against the shogun when back home in their provinces. Daimyo maintained residences for themselves and their retinues in Edo, which caused the city to grow very rapidly and to develop a local culture in which samurai largely set the tone.

Samurai had a nearly total monopoly on government posts and had various other privileges, such as the discretion to summarily execute commoners they judged to have misbehaved.[19] One can hope that wanton abuse of this authority

---

[19] For an example in fiction, see the summary of "Hunting Early Mushrooms Sows the Seeds of Love" in Gundry, *Parody, Irony and Ideology*, pp. 250–56. See also the entry on "Disrespect Killing" in Constantine Vaporis, *The Samurai Encyclopedia: A Comprehensive Guide to Japan's Elite Warrior Class* (Rutland: Tuttle, 2022), pp. 96–100.

was at least somewhat curbed by the knowledge that an individual samurai's superiors in the samurai hierarchy in turn had the power of life and death over *him*, and might lethally punish him for cavalierly cutting down commoners in the street.

Although low-ranking samurai could be quite poor, in theory they were owed deference by even the wealthiest *chōnin*. In order to suppress the consumption by affluent commoners of luxuries that made patent the discrepancy between the official hierarchy of hereditary status-group and the fluid, de facto hierarchy of wealth in an era of unprecedented economic mobility, the shogunate issued a flurry of sumptuary regulations around the time that Saikaku wrote his fiction. The fact that these edicts kept coming seems to indicate that they were largely ignored.[20] It is with this in mind that one should read the detailed cataloguing of consumer goods, services, prices and interest rates in *This Scheming World*.

The Tokugawa shogunate was a samurai regime, so of course Saikaku could not flatly condemn samurai as a class or the privileges that the shogunate granted them. This and the subtlety and ambiguity of Saikaku's fiction make a fertile topic for debate the question of whether his fiction evinces any resentment of the samurai and their prerogatives, or the limits the shogunate placed in the way of *chōnin* aspirations. This issue recalls those surrounding the interpretation of Saikaku's

---

[20] Doi Noritaka, "Shashi kinshi to ken'yakurei," *Nihon rekishi*, Vol. 526 (March 1992), pp. 61–63; Gundry, "Hierarchy, Hubris, and Parody," p. 357; Gundry, *Parody, Irony and Ideology*, pp. 16–17; Hibbett, *Floating World*, pp. 4, 6–7, 25; Donald Keene, *World Within Walls* (New York: Columbia University Press, 1999), p. 200; Donald H. Shively, "Sumptuary Regulation and Status in Early Tokugawa Japan," *Harvard Journal of Asiatic Studies*, Vol. 25 (1964–1965), pp. 123–64; Conrad Totman, *Early Modern Japan* (Berkeley: University of California Press, 1993), pp. 136–37, 245.

fiction's forays into moral didacticism. Where some see irony in Saikaku's fiction's *chōnin*-directed narratorial moralizing others do not. One should remember that this is not an all-or-nothing game, that the mocking of moralistic texts or outlooks on life does not necessarily constitute an effort to sweep aside all morality. Likewise, it is possible to portray the Tokugawa era's ruling status-group in a manner that reflects both admiration for the samuai's bravery, cultural achievements and code of honor while also expressing disapproval of samurai abuses of power and a perceived samurai penchant for unnecessary violence, as I believe some of the stories in *Exemplary Tales of the Way of the Warrior* do, or even portraying the samurai and their ethos as obsolete.[21] As for the few appearances of samurai characters in *This Scheming World*, it is worth noting that they include a ronin extortionist and the wife who serves as his accomplice in "Pawning an Old Halberd Sheath," as well as a gang of ronin robbers in "The Kitchen Floor Parties of Nara." The wife in the former story shamelessly invokes her illustrious samurai pedigree while engaging in violent histrionics in a successful attempt to pawn a cheaply made item for much more than it is worth. In so doing she brings to mind the villain of *Way of the Warrior*'s "Hunting Early Mushroom's Sows the Seeds of Love," who pompously invokes his samurai status and his imperial ancestry as he threatens the life of the *chōnin* lover of a samurai youth whom he wants for himself.[22]

---

[21] Gundry, *Parody, Irony and Ideology*, pp. 197–262; David Gundry, "Samurai Lovers, 'Samurai Beasts': Warriors and Commoners in Ihara Saikaku's *Way of the Warrior* Tales," *Japanese Studies*, Vol. 35, Issue 2, 2015, pp. 151–68.

[22] Gundry, *Parody, Irony and Ideology*, pp. 250–56.

The Geographical Context

In Saikaku's day, the influence of the imperial court aristocracy on the local culture of Kyoto through both example and the luxury industries it supported continued to give the city and its people a reputation for refinement. The culture of Osaka, the business capital of Japan, reflected the tastes of wealthy merchants. Saikaku's fiction places great emphasis on its geographical settings, and engages in much comparing and contrasting of the three great metropolises of Edo, Kyoto and Osaka, which are portrayed as the foci of, respectively, the samurai, aristocratic and mercantile varieties of cultural sophistication. Honorable mentions go to Osaka's seaport neighbor Sakai and to distant Nagasaki, made rich as the port for trade with China and the Netherlands and depicted in Saikaku's fiction as having a fascinatingly exotic local culture of which the presence of Chinese traders especially is an integral element.

Saikaku's portrayals of the rest of Japan often partake of the metropolitan contempt for provincial towns and the countryside that is a longstanding feature of East Asian cultures. One perceives this strikingly in both *The Tale of Genji* and *The Life of an Amorous Man*. In the former, the provinces are presented as places of suffering and degradation for aristocrats exiled or posted there, and their inhabitants are portrayed as disgusting boors speaking offensive, barely comprehensible dialects. *Amorous Man* contrasts the sophistication of the licensed quarters and kabuki districts of Osaka, Kyoto, and Edo, as well as the licensed quarter of Nagasaki, with the varying degrees of unsophistication and shabbiness that reign in the various provincial locales where its libidinous protagonist sam-

ples the services of the local sex industry.[23] The most prominent example of such geographical snobbery in *This Scheming
World* comes with the narrator's wry observation in "Even
Gods Make Mistakes Sometimes" that year gods "dislike having to preside over the New Year festivities in rural areas."

Nagasaki's exotic image is traceable at least as far back as
Kyushu's period of contact with Spanish and Portuguese missionaries and traders from the 1540s. Efforts begun by Hideyoshi to suppress Christianity were followed up on with a
vengeance by the new shogunate in the early 1600s, such that
remaining Iberian missionaries were expelled and Japanese
Christians were forced on pain of death to renounce their re-
ligion. Dutch traders confined to a small concession in Nagasaki became the only Westerners allowed entry into Japan,
and the presence of Chinese traders was almost as severely
limited. Japanese were forbidden to travel abroad, and were
required to register with a particular Buddhist temple in order
to help prevent the reemergence of Christianity.[24] One sees
perhaps a hint of longing for the ability to travel overseas in
"The Pillar Rice-Cakes of Nagasaki" when its protagonist
consults a Chinese merchant in that city regarding the world
beyond Japan.

Buddhism

The Buddhist emphasis on the impermanence of all phenomena and the suffering brought by attachment to any of
them—people, possessions, social status, beauty and other

---

[23] Gundry, *Parody, Irony and Ideology*, pp. 75–83.
[24] Marius B. Jansen, *The Making of Modern Japan* (Cambridge: Belknap/
Harvard University Press, 2000), pp. 66–68, 75–80.

sensual pleasures—as well as the doctrine that such attachment drives the cycle of rebirth and thus delays the attainment of the bliss of nirvana,[25] have had a profound and, paradoxically, long-lasting influence on the arts of Japan, most especially literature. Although Japan did develop a genre of Buddhist poetry focused on the supposedly nine stages of decomposition of corpses,[26] the Japanese-language poetry of the imperial court aristocracy, whose rules of word choice and topic banished the horrifying and the repulsive, prefers aesthetically pleasing examples of conspicuous impermanence—cherry blossoms, autumn leaves, dewdrops strung jewel-like on spiderwebs—and goes so far as to present their evanescence, which provides both an object lesson in Buddhist doctrine and a subtly masochistic frisson, as enhancing the pleasure of beholding them. This Buddhism-derived aestheticization of evanescence spread from Japanese court poetry, that nation's prestige literary genre par excellence, to various narrative and dramatic genres as can be seen in works ranging from Heian-period fiction such as *Tales of Ise* and *The Tale of Genji* to nō plays and the fiction of Ihara Saikaku. Over the centuries this strain in Japanese aesthetics (which to an extent was borrowed from and has counterparts in China)[27] developed new articulations in the arts and connoisseurship, such as an appreciation for the look of weathered wood or the pa-

[25] In Mahayana Buddhism, nirvana, originally conceived of as pure extinction, comes to be posited as an undefinable, unworldly bliss (Bernard Faure, *The Red Thread: Buddhist Approaches to Sexuality* [Princeton: Princeton University Press, 1998], p. 42).

[26] James H. Sanford, "The Nine Faces of Death: 'Su Tung-po's' Kuzō-shi," *The Eastern Buddhist*, Vol. 21, No. 2 (1988), pp. 54–77.

[27] Helen Craig McCullough, trans., introduction, notes, *Tales of Ise: Lyrical Episodes from Tenth-Century Japan* (Stanford: Stanford University Press, 1968), pp. 18–25 (translator's introduction).

tina of age on various manmade objects, and literature that derives much of its aesthetic appeal from an ever wider range of types of instability. This comes even to include a sort of aestheticization of false appearances born of a linguistic and conceptual conflation of the impermanent and the false that I suspect is far from self-evident to most Westerners. Mahayana Buddhism tells its adherents that since phenomena do not arise independently and inevitably morph into something else, the distinctions we perceive between phenomena are ultimately illusory. Much as the evanescence of cherry blossoms teaches the observer about the impermanence of all phenomena, places of heightened falsity such as the tinselly world of licensed prostitution quarter, where the high-end sex industry sold the illusion that the customer was entering into an uncoerced love affair with a woman who was in fact an indentured sex worker, are in texts like the first novella in Saikaku's *Five Women Who Loved Love* presented as teaching the punter about the falsity of *all* appearances. Much as Japanese court poetry encourages the appreciation of the evanescently beautiful while keeping in mind its evanescence, Saikaku's fiction portrays the fleeting pleasures of sex (especially commercial) and the enjoyment of various consumer goods not as something to shun but rather as experiences to savor in the full knowledge of their fleeting nature and thus, ultimately, of their unreality, experiences enriched by the lessons they provide regarding the unreality of the more stealthily unreal everyday phenomena that surround one.

This is the aesthetic sensibility summed up in the punning term *ukiyo*, which at first designated Buddhism's conception of a wretched (*uki*) world (*yo*) in which suffering is caused by attachment to impermanent phenomena, but came also to make use of an aesthetically pleasing homonym to the first half of the original expression meaning floating or drifting, in which case it was used both to emphasize the unstable and unpredictable nature of the entire phenomenal world and to designate the especially unstable realm of pleasure-seeking. The fiction of Ihara Saikaku and his successors over the next century or so came to be called *ukiyozōshi*, floating-world fiction. In the case of Saikaku's fiction the term is apt in that it frequently takes as its setting the worlds of prostitution and the (prostitution-connected) kabuki theater and evinces, in this and other settings, a preoccupation with an instability-falsity that as, along with eroticism, a key source of narrative interest, becomes an object of aesthetic appreciation. With its depictions of the instability in characters' economic situations, the lying, dissembling and fakery that characters use to get out of paying debts or to appear more wealthy than they really are, and occasional references to prostitution, *This Scheming World* partakes fully of the "floating world" qualities of Saikaku's fiction.[28]

The Revised Translation

Masanori Takatsuka and David C. Stubbs's original translation of *Seken mune sanyō* reads well and contains many brilliantly executed dynamic equivalents to difficult passages in the classical Japanese of the source text. Their translation also goes to greater lengths to familiarize the contents of its stories for English-speaking readers than is currently fashionable among translators of Japanese literature, which makes for a number of incongruous juxtapositions of the Japanese and the Western. I found it jarring, for example, to use the word "farthing" in a

---

[28] Gundry, *Parody, Irony and Ideology*, pp. 30–37, 118–23.

text that also makes ample reference to Japanese units of currency used in Saikaku's day. I have no doubt that in much of the English-speaking world there has been a deplorable decline since 1965 in the public's knowledge of the culture of ancient Greece, such that having a passage in the translation say that a talkative character in "How Lovely the Sight of the Rice-Cake Flowers at New Year's" was nicknamed "Demosthenes" makes less sense now than it might have then. So I have eliminated "farthing" and restored the original nickname of the chatty character, adding that he is so named "after the Buddha's most eloquent disciple." Likewise, in "How Lovely the Sight" I have changed a comparison of bill collectors to "wing-footed Mercuries" back to a reference to the swift-footed Buddhist guardian deity Idaten, and so on. I judge the retention of Buddhist references to be especially important as they make it easier for English-speaking readers to perceive the Buddhistic tone that is integral to Saikaku's fiction.

I have not been absolutely consistent in my elimination of expressions tied to specific aspects of Western culture; although I held "farthing" to be too specifically British and too noticeably un-Japanese, "penny-pincher" struck me as close to universal in English-speaking countries and as drawing less attention to itself, though a case could be made for replacing it with "miser" or "skinflint." I have attempted to avoid conspicuous Americanisms as well as chiefly British vocabulary uncommon in North America. I have also tried to steer clear of words and expressions that are obviously of recent vintage, but I have also used words that I know were not part of the English language when these stories were written in the 1680s. I have never heard anyone of any nationality refer to "sea ears" in a culinary or any other context, and have not seen the term used in contemporary texts except when given as a synonym for "abalone," so I have substituted the latter for the former, even though the Oxford English Dictionary tells me that it is chiefly used in the United States and entered the English language in the 1800s.

The original translators opted to call months by English names, referring to the first month of pre-Meiji Japan's lunar calendar, which originated in China, "January," the second month "February" and so forth. East Asian Lunar New Year occurs in late January or early February, which means that readers of the original translation will imagine seasonal settings that are about one month out of sync with those of the original. Six of the twelve English month names also have the disadvantage being derived from the names of Roman deities and emperors, which in the context of these stories creates a dissonance similar to that caused by references to Mercury and Demosthenes. For these reasons I have translated the months of the year as "the first month," "the second month," and so on, which is in any case now the standard practice for translations of pre-Meiji Japanese texts.

According to the system of age-reckoning of premodern and early-modern Japan, people were one year old at birth and became a year older on each New Year's Day, rather than on their birthdays. This meant that someone born on New Year's Eve counted as a year older than someone born one day later. Subtracting a year of age in an English translation would give an accurate picture of the age of the person born on New Year's Day but not, to take the most extreme example, of the person born the day before, so in this revised translation the ages are left as they are in the original classical Japanese text, as is also the case in the original translation.

I have compared the 1965 translation line by line to Jinbō Kazuya's thoroughly annotated edition of the original in volume 68 of Shōgakukan's *Shinpen Nihon koten bungaku zenshū*. In the case of vague, ambiguous or otherwise difficult passages, I also consulted Jinbō's parallel modern Japanese translation at the bottom of the page, as well as the separate modern Japanese translation by the venerable Saikaku scholar Teruoka Yasutaka.[29] In so doing I found numerous places where the 1965 English translation diverged substantially from the original as explicated by Jinbō and as rendered in modern Japanese by both Jinbō and Teruoka, thus necessitating changes. For example, the baby of the couple in "Golden Dreams" is gendered as male in the 1965 English translation, presumably because the child is referred to early on with the term *segare*, which in modern Japanese is used to refer to sons. The original story later indicates that the child in question is female. An annotation by Jinbō clarifies this apparent inconsistency by noting that at the time the story was written *segare* was used to refer to both boys and girls. To give another example, in describing the appearance of certain beggars who play a role in Nagasaki's New Year's celebrations, the original uses wording directly translatable as "they make their faces red," and the 1965 translation interprets this as indicating that their faces are "flushed with *sake*." However, an annotation by Jinbō observes that the beggars in question customarily painted their faces red on this occasion, and both his modern Japanese translation and Teruoka's reflect this. The 1965 translation does not indicate the Japanese edition or editions that Takat-

---

[29] Ihara Saikaku, *Seken mune san'yō*, in Taniwaki Masachika, Teruoka Yasutaka, Jinbō Kazuya, eds, *Shinpen Nihon koten bungaku zenshū*, Vol. 68: *Ihara Saikaku shū 3* (Tokyo: Shōgakukan, 1996), pp. 333–474 (henceforth referred to as *SNKBZ*); Ihara Saikaku, trans. Teruoka Yasutaka, *Gendaigoyaku Saikaku zenshū*, Vol. 11: *Seken mune san'yō, Yorozu no fumi hōgu* (Tokyo: Shōgakukan, 1976).

suka and Stubbs used, so I do not know to what extent these were annotated, and thus have deferred to the authority of Jinbō and Teruoka in cases like those described above.

Some romanizations in this translation have been changed to make them conform to current conventions in transcribing Japanese. Macrons were added to long vowels in romanizations of Japanese words that have not been adopted into English, as well as to proper nouns other than place names that are commonly referenced in English texts. I have made a few changes to wording that I simply judged infelicitous, with a humble awareness that these decisions are inherently arbitrary. Other small changes were necessary to hide the seams connecting Takatsuka and Stubbs's language with mine and to aim for a consistent style throughout the revised translation. I am grateful to both these translators for their creation of a compelling rendering of the original text, and to Professors Jinbō and Teruoka and other Japanese scholars for the painstaking philological work that has allowed me, I believe, to make this revised edition of the translation more accurately reflect the original work.

David J. Gundry
University of California, Davis, May 2023.

Suggestions for Further Reading

Drake, Christopher. "Saikaku's Haikai Requiem: *A Thousand Haikai Alone in a Single Day*, The First Hundred Verses." *Harvard Journal of Asiatic Studies*, Vol. 52, No. 2 (December 1991).

Gundry, David J. "Hierarchy, Hubris, and Parody in Ihara Saikaku's *Kōshoku ichidai otoko*." *The Journal of Japanese Studies*, Vol. 43, No. 2, Summer 2017, pp. 355–87.

Gundry, David J. *Parody, Irony and Ideology in the Fiction of Ihara Saikaku*. Leiden: Brill, 2017.

Gundry, David. "Samurai Lovers, 'Samurai Beasts': Warriors and Commoners in Ihara Saikaku's *Way of the Warrior Tales*." *Japanese Studies*, Vol. 35, Issue 2, 2015, pp. 151–68.

Hibbett, Howard. *The Floating World in Japanese Fiction*. New York: Oxford University Press, 1959.

Ihara Saikaku. *Excerpts From Life of a Sensuous Man, An Episodic Festschrift for Howard Hibbett, Episode 25*, trans. Chris Drake, John Solt, Lucy North. Hollywood: Highmoonoon, 2010.

Ihara Saikaku. *Five Women Who Loved Love*, trans. Wm. Theodore de Bary. Rutland, VT: Tuttle, 1956.

Ihara Saikaku. *The Great Mirror of Male Love*, trans. Paul Gordon Schalow. Stanford, CA: Stanford University Press, 1990.

Ihara Saikaku. *The Japanese Family Storehouse*, trans. G.W. Sargent. London: Cambridge University Press, 1959.

Ihara Saikaku. *The Life of an Amorous Woman and Other Writings*, trans. Ivan Morris. New York: New Directions, 1963.

Ihara Saikaku. *Some Final Words of Advice*, trans. Peter Nosco. Rutland, VT: Tuttle, 1980.

Ihara Saikaku. *Tales of Samurai Honor*, trans. Caryl Ann Callahan. Tokyo: *Monumenta Nipponica*, 1981.

Ihara Saikaku. *Worldly Mental Calculations: An Annotated Translation of Ihara Saikaku's Seken munezan'yō*, trans. Ben Befu. Berkeley: University of California Press, 1976.

Jansen, Marius B. *The Making of Modern Japan*. Cambridge, MA: Belknap/Harvard University Press, 2000.

Johnson, Jeffrey. "The Carnivalesque in Saikaku's Œuvre," in Jeffrey Johnson, ed., *Bakhtinian Theory in Japanese Studies*. Lewiston, NY: The Edwin Mellen Press, 2001.

Jones, Sumie; Kern, Adam L.; Watanabe, Kenji, eds. *A Kamigata Anthology: Literature from Japan's Metropolitan Centers, 1600–1750*.

Keene, Donald. *World Within Walls: Japanese Literature of the Pre-modern Era 1600–1867*. New York: Columbia University Press, 1999.

Kornicki, Peter. *The Book in Japan: A Cultural History from the Beginnings to the Nineteenth Century*. Honolulu: University of Hawai'i Press, 2001.

Leupp, Gary P. *Male Colors: The Construction of Homosexuality in Tokugawa Japan*. Berkeley: University of California Press, 1995.

Moretti, Laura. "*Kanazōshi* Revisited: The Beginnings of Japanese Popular Literature in Print." *Monumenta Nipponica*, Vol. 65, No. 2 (2010), pp. 297–356.

Pflugfelder, Gregory M. *Cartographies of Desire: Male-Male Sexuality in Japanese Discourse, 1600-1950*. Berkeley: University of California Press, 1999.

Shirane, Haruo, ed., introductions, and commentary. *Early Modern Japanese Literature: An Anthology, 1600–1900*. New York: Columbia University Press, 2002.

Vaporis, Constantine Nomikos. *The Samurai Encyclopedia: A Comprehensive Guide to Japan's Elite Warrior Class*. Rutland, VT: Tuttle, 2022.

Varley, Paul. *Japanese Culture*. Honolulu: University of Hawai'i Press, 2000.

Preface

ARLY in the morning on New Year's Day in this peaceful reign of the Tokugawa, even the wind in the pines[1] is quiet. One can make out the cries of a vendor of printed paper images of a young Ebisu, god of fortune, which merchants all buy for good luck in business. In succeeding days they engage in various annual observances: the binding of a new account book for the New Year, taking inventory, the opening and inspection of the money vault. The first time in the year that a merchant weights money, it is as if the little hammer he uses to stabilize his scale becomes the god of wealth Daikoku's magic mallet, which can produce whatever he who wields it desires. Likewise, if only he draws

---

[1] The mention of pines is an oblique but easily recognizable reference to the Tokugawa shogunal dynasty, which originated from the Matsudaira clan, the name of which begins with the word for "pine." The Tokugawa are not directly mentioned here. Expressions of gratitude toward the Tokugawa are a typical feature of the opening passages of Saikaku's works of fiction. (*SNKBZ* p. 337 note 1.)

on his own store of wisdom, every merchant can earn what he wishes. For this reason, from New Year's Day onward a merchant must tirelessly calculate the likely outcome of his business decisions and prepare for the final day of the year, when debts are settled, a day that is worth a thousand pieces of gold.

(First month of the year of the monkey, the fifth year of the Genroku era.)[2]

---

[2] 1692.

This Scheming World

The Extravagant Wives
of Wholesalers

I T IS the way of the world that on New Year's Eve the night is dark.[1] Ever since the remote ages of the gods people have been clearly aware of this truth; yet they are always neglecting their business. Much to their embarrassment, they frequently find the result of their previous calculations to be all too short to tide them over the year end. This is due entirely to their ill-advised way of living.

The year end is more precious than a mint of money. It is the Great Divide between winter and spring, which none can pass over without paying a heavy toll. It is too high to be climbed by those who labor under a load of debt, which commonly results from their fond wish to provide for their children according to their means. Each separate expenditure amounts to little or nothing at the time, but the sum total for the year is quite overwhelming. The toy bow and arrow will soon be thrown into the dust bin, and even the ball of thread

---

[1] I.e., because of when it falls during the lunar month.

quickly becomes threadbare. The toy mortar used for the
Dolls' Festival will be broken and the gilded wooden sword of
the Boys' Festival will soon fade. The drum used in the Obon
dance will be split with too much beating, while the toy sparrows of the Rice Festival, together with the stalks of Job's tears
from which they are suspended, will be cast aside. Furthermore, in observance of the second day of the Boar, rice cakes
must be prepared, as well as dumplings for the festival of the
community god. Then on the first day of the twelfth month
coppers must be offered to exorcise the devils, and a talisman
bought to neutralize the effects of ominous dreams. All these
and other such things cost money, and they pile up in such
abundance that no treasure boat nor single cart could hold
them all.

In recent years, moreover, almost all housewives have
waxed extravagant. Although not in the least short of kimono,
they have to have another one of the very latest fashion for the
New Year. It must be made as elaborately as possible: of silk
that costs forty-five *monme* of silver per half *hiki*; dyed a thousand delicate tints and hues, with as many varied and intricate
designs; and costing, possibly, a *ryō* of gold. In this way money
is squandered on what does not really attract much attention.
The obi will be of old imported satin made with genuine silk,
twelve feet long and two feet wide, costing two pieces of silver.
The hair comb may cost two *ryō* of gold, but wouldn't a
woman balancing three *koku* of rice on top of her head attract
more attention? The petticoats must be made of crimson silk,
worn in duplicate, and white *tabi* are *de rigueur*.

In olden times, even the ladies of the mightiest lords were
strangers to any such luxury. If these modern wives of merchants would only pause a moment to consider, they would
realize that divine retribution is bound to fall upon them. It

may be excusable to some extent for a woman of means to indulge in such extravagancies. However, if her merchant husband is in debt up to his ears, with interest breeding continually, day and night, rain or shine, it is not a burden to be shrugged off lightly.

Rather should the wife be more prudent, and be thoroughly ashamed of herself for indulging in such luxuries. Is it barely possible that she is laying in a supply of expensive stuff against the day when her husband, who may be even now teetering on the brink of bankruptcy, will be completely ruined? After all, women's possessions are exempt from attachment: maybe the wife means to pawn the goods to raise money. However, generally speaking, a woman is so shallow-pated that even on the very eve of her husband's bankruptcy she will fare forth in a sedan chair, attended by two men each bearing a lantern, a quite superfluous accessory in the moonlight. Her actions are as vain and futile as wearing rich brocade in the dark, or as silly as taking the trouble to heat the bath then not getting in until it's gone cold.

From his place of enshrinement within the household altar, the deceased father witnesses this procession of follies. Though sorely vexed, it's useless to admonish his son and heir, the current master of the household, for the two are living in entirely different worlds. Yet to himself he says: "My son's business is basically unsound. He buys ten *kan* worth of goods and sells them for eight *kan*. This kind of so-called 'business management' results in nothing but the decrease of capital. By the end of the year it's inevitable that an auction notice will be posted on his door. It will announce that this house of ninety-foot frontage, including three strong rooms, will be sold at auction to the highest bidder, together with all its furniture and mats (both high-and middle-class) numbering two hundred and forty in all, along with an intercoastal vessel and a five-passenger pleasure craft, plus a small rowboat, the said auction to be held on the nineteenth day of the first month of the coming year, at the town hall."

Thus will all the son's property fall into the hands of others, all of which the father foresees with deep regret. He likewise discerns, beyond a shadow of a doubt, that the paraphernalia used in the Buddhist religious services will also pass into other hands. Therefore he appears to his son in a dream with a timely warning:

"That trio of bronze treasures is among our dearest family heirlooms," he says, "much too precious to pass into the hands of outsiders. I'll have to have them wrapped up in a lotus leaf, to take back with me to Paradise in the seventh month when you light the *Obon* Fire to speed my parting spirit. After all, the inherited business of this house won't survive the year end. When you bought that considerable parcel of rice land in Tanba Province, my boy, you probably realized that yourself, didn't you, thinking to provide a place of retreat? Actually, however, that transaction was nothing but a piece of indiscretion. If you think you're so smart, just remember that the man who finances you is no less clever. Nothing will escape his scrutiny, and no alternative remains for you; everything will pass into the hands of strangers. Instead of playing the fool— and that to no purpose—why don't you apply yourself to business? Even though I'm dead, my son, I have appeared to you in this dream because I love you." Thus spoke the deceased father.

The dream passed, the morning of the twenty-ninth day of the twelfth month dawned, and the young merchant awoke, shaking with laughter in his bed. "Dear, oh dear!" he exclaimed. "To see the old gentleman in a dream just at this busy year end! How perfectly shocking to discover that my dead father is still so grasping that even in the other world he wants me to donate that trio of treasures to the temple."

But even as he spoke so disparagingly of his deceased father the creditors came pouring in, one after another. How was he to meet the situation?

Well, in recent days, merchants short of money have originated the idea of a so-called bill of exchange, or draft. Whenever they can spare the cash, they deposit it with a bill broker without interest, on condition that when the need arises he will pay it out for them. A rather clever device it is, convenient alike to both creditor and borrower. Our young merchant likewise, making use of this new system, had deposited twenty-five *kan* of silver with a trusted broker toward the end of the eleventh month. When the time for the general settlement of debts arrived at the year end, he handed one draft to the rice dealer, another to the draper, a third to the miso dealer, a fourth to the fishmonger—indeed, to each and every creditor who came along he made out a draft, saying it would be cashed by his broker. He even paid his dues to the Kannon Worship Society with a draft, as well as his bills from the house of assignation.[2]

Then, proclaiming that all had been attended to, he pushed off for Sumiyoshi Shrine, to spend the last night of the old year in calm, unruffled prayer. Yet the waves in his bosom never ceased to roll. Perhaps the god of Sumiyoshi felt somewhat uneasy about accepting gifts from such a fellow.

Now whereas the drafts he had drawn on the broker totaled eighty *kan* of silver, only twenty-five *kan* was on deposit.

---

[2] An establishment in the licensed prostitution quarter to which prostitutes were summoned to entertain customers.

Hence the broker announced that since there were too many bills to be cleared, none would be cashed until all the other accounts had been duly settled. While the broker was inquiring more carefully into the matter, the drafts were wafted about from one creditor to another, until at last the confusion was so thorough that none could tell who had which draft. The end result was that they were forced to speed the parting old year with dishonored bills on hand.

Then came the dawn! The dawn of a truly auspicious New Year.

Pawning an Old Halberd Sheath

A SOLAR eclipse occurred on New Year's Day sixty-nine years ago,[1] and when again on the selfsame day in the fifth year of Genroku another occurred, people witnessed a most uncommon dawn of the New Year. As for the calendar, in the fourth year of the reign of Empress Jitō, there was inaugurated the Gihō Calendar, which was based upon the eclipses of the sun and moon. Ever since then the people have trusted the calendar.

Now, the days moved quickly by, one after another, from the top of the calendar to the bottom, until at last they reached the nethermost rung. It is then that people become so busily occupied that not a sound can be heard—not a tune—not even a hum. In the poorer quarters particularly they find it necessary to quarrel, to wash, and to repair the foundations of the walls all at the same time. The result is that they lack time to prepare for the New Year. Not one piece of rice cake, nor

---

[1] There is no record of this eclipse (*SNKBZ* p. 346 note 1).

even a dried sardine, do they have. Poor and miserable indeed is their life when compared with that of the rich. How in the world do they manage to tide over the year end, these people who are crowded into half a dozen or more narrow sections of a single tenement-house?

Because each of them has something or other to pawn, they show no signs of anxiety. With the one exception of rent, which is paid at the end of each month, they are accustomed every day of their lives to buy for cash whatever necessities of life they may need, such as rice, miso, firewood, vinegar, soy sauce, salt, oil, and the like; for nobody will sell them anything on credit. So when the end of the month comes, no creditor will slip up on them unannounced with his account book open, nor is there anyone for them to be afraid of, or anyone to whom they must apologize for unpaid bills. In their case, the saying of the old sage indeed holds true: "Pleasure lies in poverty."

People who refuse to pay their debts are no better than daylight burglars in disguise. In brief, because they make only a very rough estimate for the year, not figuring their income and outgo month by month, most people find their income insufficient to make both ends meet. But in the case of people who live from hand to mouth things are different. Can they improve their lot by taking pains to enter their expenditures in an account book? Why, even on the very eve of the New Year their daily life is not a bit different from what it is the other days of the year. How is it possible in such circumstances for them to celebrate the New Year? Their only expectation, poor chaps, lies in their pawning whatever they may happen to have at hand.

For example, one of them will pawn an old umbrella, a cotton gin and a teakettle, which enables him to have one *monme* of silver with which to tide over the season. As for the chap who lives next door to him, the pawnable articles he finds are his wife's everyday *obi* (she will make paper string do), his cotton hood, a set of picnic lunch boxes with the top lid missing, a weaving frame three hundred threads wide, a five-*gō* and a one-*gō* measure, five porcelain dishes manufactured in Minato, and a hanging scroll painting of Amida Buddha with assorted ritual implements—a grand total of twenty-three items in all, for which he receives the magnificent sum of one *monme* and six in silver to get through the year end.

The neighbor living to the east of him is a dancing beggar, who during the New Year season is accustomed to switch to the Daikoku dance. Since an appropriate mask costing five *mon* and a papier-mâché mallet will suffice for the season, unnecessary are his headgear, his dancing kimono, and his hakama. So these he will pawn for two *monme* and seven, and thus pass the year end in tranquility.

Next door to him lives a trouble-making ronin who wears only paper clothes, for he has long since sold off his weapons and harness to buy food. Hitherto he has managed to scrape out a bare living by making toy fishing tackle, using the hairs from horses' tails. But as these are now passé, he is quite reduced to want and is at a complete loss as to how to tide over the year end. Finally, in desperation he sends his wife to the pawnbroker's with their old halberd sheath. No sooner has the pawnbroker picked it up, however, than he throws it back at the woman, remarking that it is worthless. In an instant her countenance changes and in a fit of rage she screams, "Why do you throw my precious possession about? If you won't take it in pledge, just say so! 'Worthless,' you say? Such abusive words cannot be ignored. This is the sheath of the very halberd my dead father used when he so valiantly distinguished himself at the Battle of Sekigahara. Having no son, he gave it to me, and when in better days I was married, it sheathed the very halberd in my wedding procession. To disparage it is to cast shame upon my ancestors. I'm only a woman, I know, but I'm ready this very instant to die if need be. Now I'll fight!" So saying she grabs the pawnbroker around the waist with all her might, at the same time bursting into tears. Overwhelmed with embarrassment, the pawnbroker apologizes as profusely as possible, but the angry woman is not to be so easily appeased.

Meantime the neighbors have come thronging into the shop, and one of them whispers into the pawnbroker's ear that he'd better settle the matter before word reaches the ears of her husband, for he is a notorious extortionist. So after much ado, he manages to settle the trouble by offering her three hundred *mon* in copper, plus three *shō* of unpolished rice. Alas, to what depths has she sunk. This raging woman was once the beloved daughter of a warrior whose annual stipend was twelve hundred *koku* of rice. Accustomed to an elegant lifestyle in her better days, it is only her present poverty that has driven her into such unconscionable extortion. Recollecting her illustrious past, she must have been filled with a sense of shame. From a single example such as this one, it is apparent that it just won't do for anyone to die poor!

Well, anyway, the matter now being settled, she receives the three hundred copper *mon* and the three *shō* of rice. But unpolished rice, she complains, will be useless on the morrow. "Oh, fortunately, Ma'am," replies the pawnbroker, "I happen to have a mortar right here. You are welcome to use it to polish the rice." Could this incident be cited as a good illustration of the saying, "A touch will cost you three hundred *mon*?"

Next door to the ronin lives a woman of thirty-seven or

thirty-eight years, all alone, for she has no relatives, not even a son to depend on. Her husband, she says, died several years ago; so she had her hair cut short and has worn plain clothes ever since. Yet she still cares for her personal appearance as much as ever, and she retains a definite though unostentatious air of elegance about her. She usually spends her days spinning ramie thread, just to pass the time away. Already by early in the twelfth month she has completed her preparations for the New Year: her stock of firewood will last until the second or third month; on the fish hanger hang a medium-sized yellowtail, five small porgies, and two codfish; and everything— from lacquered chopsticks and Kii-province lacquerware down to the very lids of the pots—all is brand new. She makes a year-end present of a salt mackerel to her landlord, a pair of silk-strapped sandals to his daughter, and a pair of ribbed *tabi* to his wife; while to each member of the seven households in the building where she lives she presents a rice cake and a bunch of burdock. Thus she passes the year end by discharging every social obligation. How she makes a living is her own well-guarded secret.

Next door to her live a couple of women, the younger one of whom has ears, eyes, and a nose that are not in the least bit different from those of other girls. Yet to her great sorrow she is yet unmarried. Whenever she views herself in her mirror, however, she is compelled to realize anew why no one ever takes a second look at her. The other woman, who is older, once served as a maid, prostitute and roadside tout at an inn on the Tōkaidō highway, near the town of Seki. While working there she mistreated poor guests making secret pilgrimages to the shrine at Ise who had to prepare their own food to save money, and she would pilfer their scanty supply of rice. Divine retribution overtook her while yet in this world, however, and she is now a poor mendicant nun. Pretending to be pious, she chants sutras with no feeling of devotion. A nun in form, she is but an ogre in spirit, a veritable wolf in clerical garb. So impious is she that it never even occurs to her that she ought to abstain from eating meat. Yet for the past fourteen or fifteen years she has, by the mercy of the Buddha, managed to eke out a living, only because of her black clerical robe made of hemp. For as the saying goes, "Even a sardine's head will shine if believed in." Each morning as she walks about the streets begging rice she receives alms from an average of two houses per block, which means that to gather even a single *gō* of rice she must visit as many as twenty houses. She cannot hope to garner five *gō* of rice until she has raced through at least fifty blocks. It surely takes a healthy person to be a mendicant nun!

Unfortunately, during the previous summer, she suffered a sunstroke, which necessitated her pawning the clerical robe for one *monme* and eight. Since then, as she has been unable to redeem the robe, she has lost her means of livelihood. Of course we should not jump to the conclusion that people have become any less generous in almsgiving for the sake of their souls in the afterlife. Yet now that she is without the clerical robe, she cannot expect to collect even two *gō* of rice a day; whereas formerly when wearing it she usually received five *gō*. "Twelfth-month priest and priestess" runs the well-known saying. Yes, especially in the twelfth month when people are so busy that they forget even the services in memory of their departed parents, it is no wonder that they do not care to give alms to a mendicant nun. So, with only eight *mon* in hand, she must somehow tide over the year end.

Surely no one is in a better position to understand the misery in this world than is the cheap pawnbroker who keeps shop among the poverty-stricken in the slums, a profession that is not for the soft-hearted. Indeed, even to the eyes of the casual bystander it is obvious that the year end is replete with things both sad and pitiable.

When Ise Lobsters Were as Scarce as Crimson Leaves in Springtime

DURING the New Year season it is customary to offer pine branches to the gods and to set out *Hōrai* displays consisting of various delicacies arranged on a bed of ferns. Without Ise lobsters for the latter, the celebration of the New Year seems incomplete. It occasionally happens, however, that the price of the lobsters rises so high that a poor man or a penny-pincher has to celebrate the New Year without any.

A few years ago, when the supply of bitter oranges was so short that a single orange cost four or five *bu*, many people substituted *kunenbo* mandarin oranges, which were all right because they closely resemble bitter oranges in shape and color. However, in the case of Ise lobsters, to use a prawn as a substitute would be no more fitting than to wear borrowed clothes, but some are forced to make do with them.

The man who lives in a lofty mansion and has a reputation to uphold often finds that the winds of the world blow against his house so much harder that ordinary straw matting cannot protect his walls from the rain. It is only natural for him to cover them with wainscoting painted with persimmon tannin mixed with lamp black. For him this is no luxury, but a necessity. It's really no pleasure at all unless you eat, and dress, and live in a house in a style that accords with your means.

I might add, incidentally, that very few men have ever succeeded, whatever their business, when they altered the inherited way of managing it and ventured on some new enterprise. It is better to take the advice of the old veterans. No matter how talented a young man may be, it often happens that in the end his advance calculations are completely frustrated.

Now in Osaka the year-end scene resembles nothing so much as a treasure mart. People there are always complaining aloud that business has been bad. Actually, however, for the past sixty years they have never had to throw anything away because it hasn't been sold. Even stone mortars, which last a lifetime and can even be passed on down to posterity, are sold so regularly every day, year in and year out, that there's danger that Granite Mountain, from which the stone they are made of is quarried, will eventually disappear.

If this be true of stone mortars, it seems only natural that such seasonal things as the offerings for the *Obon* Festival in the seventh month, the toy helmets used in the Boys' Festival in the fifth month, and the things used in celebration of the New Year—all of which last but a few days—should be prepared anew each year when the proper season rolls around. Gift fans presented by temples to their parishioners are thrown away without ever having been unwrapped. No one seems even to be conscious of such a wasteful way of living. Indeed, as free spenders the citizens of Osaka are second only to the people of Edo.

Now this particular year of which I write it happened that

everyone in the city, vowing that his New Year decorations would be incomplete without an Ise lobster, determined to buy one even if it cost a thousand *kan*. The result was that by the twenty-seventh or twenty-eighth of the twelfth month the supply of Ise lobsters was so exhausted that in every fishmonger's shop in Osaka they were as scarce as imported articles. And by New Year's Eve not even a whiff of one was to be detected, high or low; all along the shore and in every fisherman's hut you could hear the plaintive voices of buyers asking if there were any Ise lobsters for sale.

At a fishmonger's shop called the Era, located in the middle of Bingo Street in Osaka, there happened to be just one Ise lobster left. The bidding for it began at one and a half *monme* and finally rose to four *monme* and eight. Even at that exorbitant price, however, the fish monger refused to part with it, claiming that its like could not be found anywhere else.

Since it was far beyond his authority to buy it at such an inflated price on his own responsibility, a servant who had gone there in search of a lobster returned home hastily to his master and explained the situation. Whereupon the master frowned and said: "Never in my life have I bought anything that was too expensive. I make it a rule to buy firewood in the sixth month, cotton in the eighth month, rice before the saké-brewing season starts, and hempen cloth just after the *Bon* season. In brief, my principle is to buy for cash when the price is cheapest. The only exception (and one which I have ever since remembered with regret) was made when my father died: I bought an expensive coffin at the price quoted by the cooper. There is no reason in the world why, willy-nilly, we should have to greet the New Year with an Ise lobster installed in our house. I'll make up for its absence this year by buying two of them some year when the price comes down to only

WHEN ISE LOBSTERS WERE AS SCARCE AS CRIMSON

three *mon* apiece. I don't mind in the least if due to the absence of an Ise lobster the New Year god is reluctant to visit my house. No, not in the least! I wouldn't buy one if the price were reduced to four *monme*—no, not even if it were only four *bu!*"

Despite the master's wry face, his wife and son both thought it just wouldn't do at all to be without an Ise lobster. They could bear up under the thought of losing face publicly, but when the daughter's husband would make his first New Year's call on his wife's parents and see no Ise lobster crowning the New Year decorations that scene was simply unthinkable. They must have one at any cost. Back went the servant post-haste, but he was too late, for another servant of a wholesaler from Imabashi had already bought the Ise lobster. The price quoted had been five *monme* and eight, but since it was appropriate to usher in the New Year with round figures, an even five hundred *mon* had been paid for it. The last lobster having been sold, then, all further forays of the servant to hunt lobsters were fruitless; so he had to return home, empty-handed, a sadder but wiser man, more conscious than ever of the great size of Osaka, and confess all to his master and mistress.

The mistress looked sorrowful, but the master laughed and said: "I feel uneasy about any wholesaler who would buy a lobster at so fancy a price. He's bound to go bankrupt before long. His financial backer, unaware of his real circumstances, is sure to have a nightmare over the holiday season. If a lobster is indispensable for the decoration, I have an idea for making one that will keep much longer than a live one." So saying, he commissioned an artisan to fashion a lobster of papier-mâché and crimson silk, which cost him only two and a half *monme*. "Look," he pointed out, "it will be useful as a toy for the baby even after the season is all over. That's the way a wise man does things. A thing that would have cost you four *monme* and eight has been provided for two and a half *monme*. And what's more, it can be used over and over again."

Since there was no gainsaying the master's proud boast, everyone was forced to listen to him and acknowledge the rare wisdom of one who could attain to such wealth as he possessed.

While all this was going on, the master's old mother, who was ninety-two years of age, but was still able to see well and to walk as well as ever, entered the room from her quarters in the annex. "I hear that you're making a lot of fuss over the price of a lobster," she remarked.

"It was foolish of you not to have bought one ahead of time. With such negligence how in the world can you expect to keep this household going? You should remember that in years when the Spring Festival comes right before the New Year lobsters are always expensive, not only because the Grand Shrine at Ise, its subordinate shrines and the households of its underling priests all need lobsters, but also because at this season there are millions of them in demand by every household in every town and countryside that holds a festival to the gods—and truly Ise province is a land of the gods! The lobsters brought into Kyoto and Osaka each year are those left over, after the gods have had their fill. Now it just happens that I took all this into consideration and about the middle of the month I bought two lobsters as fresh and natural as they came out of the sea. Perfect specimens: even their feelers have never been broken and had to be joined together. And the price I paid for them? Just four *mon* apiece, you see."

Admiring applause greeted the old mother's announcement, but some ventured to criticize her extravagance in buying two lobsters when really one would have done. "I don't spend my money to no purpose, she retorted. "There's a man who every year presents me with five bundles of burdock—three, if the burdock is thick—and I must give him in return something of like value. My plan was to give him a lobster that cost me four *mon* in return for the burdock which ought to be worth about one *monme*. It's pretty lucky for you that he hasn't come yet with his usual year-end present. I tell you what I'll do: I'll let you have one of my lobsters, but remember that business is business even between mother and son. If you really want the lobster, then you'll have to send somebody to me with five bundles of burdock. I don't care who gets the lobster, just so long as I get my burdock in exchange for it. And anyway, you can't celebrate the New Year without it. Not that I'm speaking from any selfish motive, understand. It's just that in giving and receiving presents on the five annual festival days you have to make rather careful calculations of what you receive. In return, you have to give things which, while seeming to be equal in value, actually allow you a slight margin of profit.

"For example, every year the Ise priests present our family with a box of amulets, a set of dried bonito, a box of face powder, a folding calendar, and five bundles of green laver. If you make a close calculation of their value it comes to about two *monme* and eight. Now from our house we always used to offer three *monme*, which meant that the difference of two odd *bu* represented a profit for the Grand Shrine of Ise. For thirty years this was our practice, but since you've become master of this house, each year you have offered one piece of silver. That's unconscionably too much!—even if it is an act of devotion. Why, even the shrine gods themselves would frown with disapproval upon anyone who spent money without due consideration. Take for example that offertory coin called a Pigeon's Eye. Contrary to what most people think, one *kan* of these round lead coins with a hole in the middle is actually worth only six hundred *mon*. From this it is quite apparent that the gods themselves are concerned that pilgrimages be made with due economy."

No matter how we look at it, this whole world is filled with greed. Of all the hundred and twenty subordinate shrines of Ise, the two which enjoy the richest offerings are those of Ebisu and Daikoku. Taga is the god of long life, Sumiyoshi the guardian of boatmen, and Izumo the deity of go-betweens. The god of Kagami Shrine, with its pair of sacred mirrors, makes girls look pretty; while Sannō is the chief of twenty-one minor deities. Inari is the god who sees to it that property does not pass out of the family. Or at least so claim the shrine "sparrows," those mercantile henchmen of the various gods, who chirp their praises to visitors to their shrines.

But never mind. Because they are all gods who possess some pleasing attribute, people make offerings to them. But all about the shrines of the other gods there hangs a pall of solemn loneliness. In view of the fact that we are living in an age when even the gods cannot earn money without exerting themselves, it follows as a matter of course that human beings ought never to be caught off guard.

It is a custom of the priests at the Grand Shrine at Ise to send out New Year's greetings to their devoted patrons all over the land. Since this calls for the writing of a large number of letters, skilled calligraphers who are paid one *mon* per letter are employed to write them. From one New Year's Day to the next they are busy writing the same letters over and over again, but all year long they never manage to earn even two hundred *mon* in a day. Why do they engage in such an occupation? For the sake of the everlasting prosperity which springs from the divine virtue, for the peace of the people, for the sake of devotion, and last but not least, to earn a livelihood.

The Mouse Messenger

THERE once lived a man whose invariable practice it was to clean house every thirteenth of the twelfth month. From the family temple he would receive twelve dwarf bamboo poles. He preferred the number twelve because it was a lucky one, symbolizing the months of the year. Anything connected with such an auspicious occasion as the year end has to be related to a lucky number. After using them to clean up around the house, he would use the stocks of the poles to reinforce his thatched roof. As for the twigs, he would affix them to a broom head, thus making certain that no part of the lucky bamboo should be disposed of as useless. Such was the unvarying habit of this parsimonious fellow.

Last year he was so busy on the thirteenth of the twelfth month that he postponed his house-cleaning until New Year's Eve, at which time he also prepared a hot bath, for the first and the last time of the year. It was in connection with this that he customarily utilized the waste leaves of the *chimaki* dumplings eaten in the fifth month, the lotus leaves left from the *Bon* season, and other miscellaneous odds and ends that he'd saved up to use as fuel to heat the bath. In his opinion there was no need to be particular about the type of fuel consumed, just so long as it heated the bath water. Not wishing to be wasteful in the least, he was extremely careful about even the minutest matters. His aged mother lived in the cottage annex, built to the rear of his house, and as might well be expected of the woman who had given birth to such a skinflint as he, she was as stingy as stingy could be. As she, too, was about to add fuel to the bath firebox by throwing in one odd lacquered *geta* she was reminded of her past. "The pair of *geta* of which this was the fellow," she sighed audibly, "were first brought to this house in my bridal chest when I was married at the age of eighteen. Ever since then I have worn them every day, in rain or snow. Though the undersupports have worn out several times, they've stayed in good condition all these fifty-three years. I had hoped they would last me until I died, but to my great regret one of them was carried off by a stray dog the other day. This single one isn't much good by itself, so I've got to burn it for fuel."

So complaining time and again, she tossed the lone *geta* into the firebox. But this very action brought painful memories of still another regrettable incident. So again she began complaining and bewailing the fact that "in this world the months and days pass by like so many dreams." "The first anniversary will come around tomorrow," she moaned, "to make me sad all over again."

A physician who lived in her neighborhood happened to be taking his bath. "Stop your grieving," he called out to her. "The year end is an auspicious occasion. Incidentally, who was it that died a year ago for whom you will be observing an anniversary?" he inquired.

"I'm just a foolish old woman," she answered, "but when human beings die I don't grieve so much for them, because everybody must die sooner or later. What really makes me sad is this: last New Year's Day my sister from Sakai paid me a New Year's call and brought me a present of some money. I was so happy that I at once placed it on the shelf dedicated to the god of the New Year. But that same night it was stolen. No outsider could have taken it. When all my prayers, first to this god and then to that, went unanswered, I asked *a yamabushi*[1] to perform a divination for me. He said that if the sacred paper on the altar shook and the sacred light gradually died out, it would signify that the missing money would be restored within seven days. Sure enough, the paper did begin to shake and the light went out. So deeply was I moved by this divine manifestation, which seemed to me proof that the world was not yet hopelessly degenerate, that I gave the *yamabushi* all of a hundred and twenty *mon*. After that I waited for seven days, but the money never turned up.

"I was telling this to another man, and he said that what I had done was just like throwing good money after bad. Nowadays, he told me, 'there are what are known as trickster *yamabushi*. For instance, they'll fix up various contrivances under the altar by means of which they can make paper dolls dance the Tosa dance. This is not at all new,' he continued, 'but was originally performed by a magician by the name of Matsuda. People nowadays are highly sophisticated, but for that very reason they sooner fall into the simplest of traps. The shaking of the sacred paper,' he went on, 'is caused by loaches concealed in a pot on the stand to which the paper is attached. The trickster *yamabushi* rubs his rosary and chants an incan-

---

[1] A mountain ascetic monk of the *Shugendō* branch of Buddhism.

tation, all the while wildly beating on the altar with a sacred stick. This commotion so frightens the loaches that they start darting about confusedly. When in motion they touch the wand holding the sacred paper and make it shake, striking awe into those who are not in on the trick. As for the light, in the stand there's fixed a device resembling an hourglass which drains away the supply of oil and makes the light go out.'

"When I heard this story from the man," lamented the old woman, "I realized at once that I had suffered loss upon loss. Never in my life until then had I lost even one *mon*. But now on this very New Year's Eve I find that my calculations have gone all awry. Since the money's still missing, everything looks dark for me, and I must face the New Year with a troubled spirit." So saying, the old woman burst into such a fit of unrestrained crying that it embarrassed the servants and the entire family. Furthermore, they were vexed at her suspecting them of theft, and in their hearts they swore to the various gods that they were entirely innocent.

Meantime the house-cleaning was almost done, but just as the servants reached the attic, one of them spied something wrapped up in Sugihara paper. It was the very money for which the old woman had been searching for so long a time. "You see?" they said to her. "What was never stolen is bound to turn up sooner or later. My! What a mischievous mouse that was!" But she was not to be mollified. Pounding the mats with her fists she cried out that never in her born days had she seen a mouse, or even heard of one, that could carry something that far. "I think it must have been a two-legged rat," she insisted, "so I'll still have to keep a sharp watch."

Just at this point the physician, who had just finished his bath, came over and said, "It seems to me that there are some ancient precedents that apply here. For example, on New

Year's Eve in the first year of Taika, in the reign of the thir-
ty-seventh human emperor of Japan,[2] Kōtoku, the Imperial
Residence was removed from Okamoto in Yamato to Nagara
Toyosaki in Naniwa. At the same time the mice of Yamato
also moved. Now the thing that is so fascinating is that they
carried along with them all their household effects: old cotton
to cover up their holes, paper bedclothes to shelter them from
the eyes of hawks, amulet cases to keep off the cats, pointed
pickets to block the weasel's way, things for propping open
mousetraps, wood scraps for putting out oil lamps, levers to
use when hooking dried bonito, dried abalone strips to use at
weddings, heads of dried anchovies, and bags of broken rice
for use on pilgrimages to Kumano—all these they carried
along in their mouths, throughout the entire two days' journey.
How simple then it must have been for this mouse to carry
your money so short a distance as that between the cottage
annex and the main house!" In such fashion the good physician undertook to pacify her, but his learned quotations from
ancient times were all to no avail. She still insisted that she
would not be convinced by any mere speech, no matter how
clever, but must see some concrete evidence with her own
eyes.

Everyone was perplexed as to what to do, but finally someone got the idea of bringing in a mouse-trainer named Tōbei
who had been instructed in this art by Nagasaki Mizuemon.
When he arrived they asked the old woman to watch the
mouse perform its various tricks. When Tōbei told the mouse
that a boy wanted a love letter delivered for him, it picked up
a sealed envelope in its mouth, looked all around, and then

---

[2] As opposed to the legendary first emperor of Japan, the divine Jinmu
(*SNKBZ* p. 362 note 11).

placed it in the kimono sleeve of one of the spectators. Next Tōbei threw it a one-*mon* coin, ordering it to go buy a rice cake. At once it found a rice cake and returned with it, leaving the coin in its place. "Now you are convinced, aren't you?" they asked the old woman.

"Well," she replied, "now that I have seen an actual demonstration, I don't deny that a mouse could have carried off my money. My suspicions are allayed, but it's most unfortunate that the master let such a thieving mouse stay in his house. Since it was due to his carelessness that my money was laid away for a whole year serving no useful purpose, he ought at least to pay me interest for the period of time it was missing."

So on New Year's Eve under such a pretext as this she obtained from her son interest at the rate of fifteen per cent. Then, saying that now she was in a proper mood to celebrate the arrival of the New Year, she made her way back to her lonely bed.

The One-*Monme* Society

WHEN a man becomes rich, people always say he's
lucky. But this is merely a conventional expression, for in reality he becomes rich and his household thrives solely on account of his own ability and foresight.
Even Ebisu, the god of wealth, is unable at will to exercise
power over riches.

But be that as it may, our wealthy merchants, for whom the
discussion of a pending loan to a daimyo is a far more engaging pastime than carousing or any other form of merrymaking, have recently organized themselves into a society devoted
to the deity of wealth Daikoku. Shunning a rendezvous in the
red-light district, they gather in the guest room of the Buddhist temple in Shitaderamachi or Ikutama. There they meet
every month to discuss the financial condition of each individual applicant for a loan. Though they are all well along in
years, they take pleasure only in ever-increasing interest and in
mounting capital, utterly heedless of the life to come. Although it's quite true that there's nothing more desirable than

plenty of money, the proper way for a man to get along in the world should be this: in his youth until the age of twenty-five to be ever alert, in his manly prime up to thirty-five to earn a lot of money, in the prime of discretion in his fifties to pile up his fortune, and at last in his sixties—the year before his sixty-first birthday—to turn over all his business to his eldest son. Thereafter it is proper for him to retire from active affairs and devote the remainder of his days to visiting temples for the sake of the life to come.

These wealthy merchants of the Daikoku Society, however, who have already arrived at an age when it is eminently respectable to spend their days visiting temples, continue to live in the midst of an avaricious world, completely oblivious to the way of the Buddha. Although every single one of them is worth two thousand *kan* or more, when he dies, all his property will remain in this world. He couldn't take anything along with him—except a shroud—if he possessed ten thousand *kan*.

In recent days, another less wealthy group—twenty-eight members in all—who have through their own efforts amassed only from two or three to five hundred *kan*, have formed themselves into the One-*Monme* Society. They have no regular meeting place, but wherever they gather for a meal they never order a dish that costs more than one *monme*. (Hence the name of the club.) No saké is served with the food, though all of them are not teetotalers. How suffocatingly prudent it is to be so careful of money spent even for recreation!

From morning till night the men talk of nothing but money. Principally they scrutinize this borrower or that, to decide whether or not it is safe to make him a loan, while trying also to ensure that their money does not lie idle for even one day. They have accumulated their fortunes by loaning money and battening on the interest; indeed, there's no business more profitable than money-lending. Nowadays, however, there are a goodly number of merchants who, while putting up a prosperous front, are actually hard pressed. It frequently happens that when such merchants have obtained a loan and go bankrupt, they inflict painful and unanticipated losses upon their financial backers. In spite of this, it would never do for these moneyed men to display an overweening distrust of them by outright refusal to grant them loans. "Since this is the situation," one of them begins, "let's look into the financial condition of each applicant for a loan as best we can, and then pool our information before deciding to whom we will make loans. And since all of us have agreed to this procedure, let's not try to outwit each other. Now then, just for our information, let's first of all make a list of all those who regularly borrow money from us."

To this several reply, "That's a very good idea!"

"First of all," suggests another, "let's consider Mr. So-and-so, that merchant in Kitahama. His property *in toto* is probably worth about seven hundred *kan*."

"Oh, no!" protests another. "That's wide of the mark. I happen to know that he has debts outstanding that total eight hundred and fifty *kan*."

Whereupon the entire company, being astonished that there exists such a wide discrepancy between the two opinions expressed, call for a closer inspection and ask for further details.

"The reason I believe him to be rich," volunteers one of the company, "is this: a year ago in the eleventh month his daughter married a merchant who lives in Sakai. Their bridal train stretched all the way from Imamiya to Fuji-no-maru's ointment and poultice shop in Nagamachi Street. And that's not all. That long procession was followed by five chests, carried by tall men of equal height and suspended from green bamboo poles, each chest containing ten *kan* of silver. It looked just like a shrine festival procession. This merchant has several sons in addition to the daughter. If he wasn't rich, I figured, he couldn't have given her a dowry of fifty *kan*. So, early in the fourth month I urged him to accept a loan from me of twenty *kan*, which he did with seeming reluctance."

Up spoke one of the other members of the One-*Monme* Society: "That's too bad! I'm afraid that twenty *kan* of yours will come back to you diminished to exactly one *kan* and six hundred *mon*."

Hearing him, the original speaker turned pale, paused with his chopsticks midway to his mouth, and became so agitated that he left off sipping his fish and vegetable soup. "How sad the news I hear today!" he cried, and his tears began to flow even before he had heard the substantiating details. "Please," he begged, "tell me all about it!"

"Well," replied the other man, "the father of that bridegroom is so badly in need of funds that he's willing to pay the same high interest rates that play producers have to pay. Do you know of any other business beside the theater that can afford to pay such exorbitant interest rates and remain solvent? As for those ten-*kan* chests of silver you saw in the bridal procession, you could have them duplicated—with metal fittings, too—for about three and a half *monme* apiece. The five chests probably cost him no more than seventeen and a half *monme*. There were probably stones, or broken tile, inside, or practically any old thing that weighs enough. Surely there's nothing worse than human depravity! My best guess is that those five money chests represented an effort on the part of the two households to deceive the world as to their true financial condition. As for me, even if I'd opened them up and found real silver inside I'd still not have believed it. Two hundred pieces of silver is just too much of a dowry for the daughter of a merchant who has no more money than he has. Not taking into account the value of the rest of the trousseau, I'd say that a dowry of about five *kan* would be plenty for his daughter. What do you think of my estimate? It might be best to let him have a loan of say two *kan* at first for a year or two, as a kind of test case. If the loan proves a safe one, then we may offer to lend him up to four or five *kan* for a period of some five or six years. I think that until he has proved himself to be thoroughly reliable, a loan of twenty *kan* is much too risky."

The whole company expressed their approval of his judgment. However, the man who had already made the loan of twenty *kan*, now being completely convinced by the arguments of the more experienced member of the company, became so dejected that he could hardly rise to his feet when the meeting was over. Sighing, he said: "In all my life I've never before misjudged the financial status of any man, but this time I must admit that I've been indiscreet." How, he inquired tearfully, might he recover his loan?

"There is only one safe and sure way to get your money back" replied the worldly-wise man who had just delivered the contrary judgment. "And even if you wracked your wits for a thousand days and nights, you could think of no other. For a present of one *hiki* of extra fine pongee I'll tell you how you can do it," he offered.

"That's very kind of you. I'll certainly accept that offer," answered the downcast one whose judgment had been found faulty. "Furthermore, to show my gratitude, I'll add padding to the pongee. Please reveal the secret to me."

"First of all," replied the man of wisdom, "you must cultivate his acquaintance more closely. Fortunately, the Tenma Boat Festival is not far off. On the twenty-fifth send your wife to view it from the stands on the riverbank. At that time let her fall into casual conversation with the wife of your merchant debtor about various household matters and spend an enjoyable day with her. Later, of course, for courtesy's sake her sons will be introduced to your wife. When they are, she must praise the second son for his handsomeness, saying something like this:

"'Oh, what intelligent-looking eyes your son has-so bright and sparkling! Forgive my rudeness, but I just can't help saying that this son of yours is like a peacock born to a kite, a veritable jewel among men. I don't mean to overpersuade you, but I'd love to have him for a son-in-law, and I say it in sober seriousness. My own daughter, though her mother obviously is a very plain person, has ordinary good looks. Besides, since she's the only child, her father has always said he'd give her a dowry of fifty *kan* when she marries. Besides, there's that three hundred and fifty *ryō* that I have for my private use. And then that corner house at Nagabori—it must be worth at least twenty-five *kan*. And I almost forgot to mention those sixty-five sets of kimono, still in as brand-new condition as the day they were made. She's the only one who can possibly inherit them in the future. How I wish this handsome son of yours could be her husband!'

"While your wife is speaking in this fashion she should be gazing longingly all the while at the son. So much for the first step. Now from time to time after that you should send presents of something or other to the merchant. Since he'll pay you back with things of approximately the same value, fear no loss in that quarter. Then at the proper moment you should have the son brought into your office to help your clerk count your cash. Let him work side by side with the clerk, weighing the coins in the scales, counting them, putting your hallmark on them, and storing them in your vaults. Keep him at this work a whole day. Then after that pick out some suitable person who has connections with his father in some way or other and invite him privately to your house. When he comes, say something like this to him:

"'My wife is just dying to have that man's second son as a son-in-law, though personally I can't see exactly what there is in him that attracts her so. It's not really urgent, but at your leisure if you'd sound him out as to whether or not he's interested in having my daughter as wife for his second son, I'd appreciate it very much. I can be perfectly frank with you. So let me say right out that no matter whom she marries, she'll have a dowry of a thousand pieces of silver.'

"After that, at the proper moment, when you think that enough time has elapsed for him to pass your message along to the man in question, let him know that you want to call in your loan to him. Without a doubt he will do everything in his power to repay you; because his love of money won't let him pass up the opportunity of welcoming into his household a bride with such a generous dowry. There's no other scheme but this that'll work."

Such was the gist of the advice given by the worldly-wise member of the One-*Monme* Society to his fellow financier, and then all the club members parted company.

On New Year's Eve that same year, the man who had loaned the money to the merchant comes to the one who has advised him as to the best method of recovering his loan. Smiling all over, he taps his own head and says to him: "Thank you, thank you, thank you! It is due entirely to your good advice that just a few days ago I received not only the

principal of my loan but the interest as well. Among us mon-
ey-lenders such a resourceful man as yourself is indeed a rare
jewel." Then, as he rises to leave, he says: "You recall that when
you first advised me I promised to give you a *hiki* of pongee;
however, I trust that this will do." So saying, he sets before
him two *tan* of paper cloth manufactured at Shiraishi. As he
goes out he remarks over his shoulder, "As for that matter of
the padding, I'll deliver it after New Year's."

It's Expensive to Lie
When You're Lying Low

EVERYONE was getting his pate shaved and his hair dressed and donning holiday attire. So far as appearances went, a universal mood of festivity prevailed throughout the country in keeping with the New Year. But actually everybody was not facing the New Year in exactly the same fashion.

For example, there was one merchant who was so hard pressed that he determined not to pay any of his bills at all. On New Year's Eve, no sooner had he finished his breakfast than he put on his *haori*, and with his short sword at his side made ready to disappear temporarily. In an effort to placate his wife he said to her, "You must learn that above all the most important thing is perseverance. There will come a time," he continued, "when our circumstances will improve, and then you can ride about in a sedan chair. Remember, there's still some leftover duck meat from last night's supper. Warm it over, seasoning it with saké, and eat it. When the bill collectors come, pay them all the money there is in the house. But, mind you! Keep back one *kan* for your treasure-drawing game. When the money on hand is all gone, just let matters look after themselves, and lie in bed with your back to the bill collectors." So speaking, the fellow hurriedly left home. Is it any wonder that the man was bankrupt? Seeing his funds grow shorter day after day, he had failed to come up with any ready plan to improve the situation. Woe to the wife of such a fellow: she looks old while not yet a mother. On this day of days, when every single *mon* counted, he put two or three one-*bu* coins and about thirty *monme* of silver in his purse and set out for a teahouse to which he owed no money.

"Oh," he said to the mistress as he entered the teahouse, "you haven't settled your accounts yet, have you? Just look at all those bills, scattered about like a thousand letters. I'd say they must add up to two or three *kan*. Well, each household has its own expenses to meet, you know," he continued glibly. "Why, I've got to pay the draper alone six and a half *kan*. Pity a man whose wife is so extravagant. It would really be much better for me to get a divorce and spend on prostitutes the money it costs to keep my wife. Unfortunately, however, I can't do it because she became pregnant in the third month, and just this very morning her labor pains started. They say the baby will be born today, but even before it's born they're already making a great fuss over the choice of its swaddling clothes. They send for the wet nurse. Then midwives come— three or four of them. Then the family *yamabushi* comes to charm and change the unborn infant from a girl into a boy. On top of that they have to prepare a bellyband, a cowrie shell, and a sea horse to be held in her left hand. The family doctor is busy in the next room boiling some birth-inducing herbs. Why, they even send for stems of matsutake mushrooms, but goodness knows what they're for. Worst of all, my mother-in-law has just arrived, and she goes around poking her nose into everything, whether she's welcome or not. It's all so annoying! Fortunately for me, however, they tell me I'm not supposed to be in the house; so I just dropped in here to pass the time away. Since you know nothing about my financial situation, I'm afraid you may think I'm here to escape the bill collectors, since it's New Year's Eve. But believe you me, I'm a man who owes nothing at all to anybody in this whole neighborhood. Do you mind if I stay here until the baby is born? I'll pay you in cash. By the way, that yellowtail on the fish hanger is too small; it just won't do. Here; you'd better buy a bigger one right away." So saying, the customer plunked down a one-*bu* gold coin, which delighted the mistress no end and brought a smile on her face.

"How lucky!" she exclaimed. "I'll keep this a secret from my husband and buy an *obi* with it to satisfy a longstanding desire. It's really good luck to have such a generous customer as you to come in on New Year's Eve. It's a sure sign, I believe, we'll have good luck all next year. By the way, you're much too fine a fellow to stay here in the kitchen. Why don't you move into the regular room?" she urged him sweetly.

"Well, all right," he replied. "But just remember that I'm an awfully particular eater, altogether different from other people."

It was simply comical to see the way the mistress drew saké out of a special cask and warmed it up for him. After that, she tossed her hairpin on the floor for mat divination, and counted the number of seams from where it fell to the border of the mat, to see whether they were odd or even. Three times she tried, and each time the result came out the same, indicating for certain that the baby would be a boy. Thus the prediction of the mistress and the pure fabrication of the customer coincided perfectly.

To hum a popular song to the accompaniment of a woman's shamisen at the year end, without regard to the convenience of the neighbors, is a form of amusement permitted only in the licensed prostitution quarters. In accord with the line of the song that runs so appropriately, "Leading a life of lamenting," most people of this world, with a load of care on their minds, come to the very last day of the year, only to discover that it is much too long.

Ordinarily people regret the all too swift passage of the days, but this particular day is an exception. When it finally arrives, people usually wish just the opposite.

The woman who had been called into the inn for the customer's pleasure feigned gaiety as part of her service. Although she did not feel happy, she spoke with a smile on her face: "What a pity it is that the years flit by one after another!" she said. "Last year the arrival of the New Year was delightful to me, for I could play battledore and shuttlecock, but now I'm nineteen years old. It won't be long before I'll have to sew up the slits in my kimono sleeves and be addressed as 'mama.' I'm sorry to say that this may be the last year I'll be able to wear a *furisode*."[1]

Unfortunately for the woman, the customer had a good memory, and replied, "The last time I met you at the Hanaya[2] you were wearing kimono with round sleeves and saying you'd be nineteen that very day. That must have been about twenty years ago. So by now you must be at least thirty-nine, but you're still wearing a *furisode*. What in the world could you

---

[1] A kimono with drooping sleeves. The type of clothing worn by teenagers changed when they came of age.

[2] A teahouse in Kyoto that offered the services of prostitutes (*SNKBZ* p. 379 note 19).

have to regret? It's all to your advantage to be of small build, because it makes you look young." Thus unsparingly he reminded her of her old line of talk, while the woman could only sit quietly, with hands folded in apology. So the man gave up being particular about her age, and the two of them had a peaceful sleep in a friendly bed.

An old woman who seemed to be her mother appeared while the two were still in bed together, and called her out of the room. After mentioning one or two trivial things in conversation, the mother was then heard to remark, "Sorry to bother you, but this is the last time I'll see you." For the want of fourteen or fifteen *monme* she was on her way to drown herself, she explained. On hearing this the younger woman burst into tears. Then she stripped off the padded silk *haori* she was wearing, wrapped it in a *furoshiki*, and gave it to her mother. The man was incapable of viewing this touching scene with indifference. So before the old woman left, once more a *one-bu* coin disappeared from his purse.

Feeling in high spirits after this bit of charity, his voice correspondingly rose higher. Two young men who appeared to be the sandal-bearers of a young kabuki actor[3] happened to be nearby and recognized his voice. Whereupon they entered the room and cried out, "So here you are at last! We've been by your house several times since this morning, but each time we couldn't find you because you were out. Isn't it lucky we met you here!"

Then they transacted a bit of business with him. In the end, they relieved him of all his cash, together with his *haori*,

---

[3] Young kabuki actors also worked as male prostitutes, so the implication here is that the protagonist owes the actor in question for sexual services performed.

his short sword, and one of his kimono. "And by the fifth of the first month," they reminded him as they left, "we'll expect you to pay the balance due."

The customer, though considerably out of countenance, managed to squeeze out a rather lame excuse. "I've got to see a friend of mine who has just sent word that he needs me to help him out," he explained. "In any case, it was injudicious of me to leave home on New Year's Eve." Thus putting up a front of respectability, he left the teahouse at daybreak. As he went off, the people there laughed and said, "Why, even a fool has more sense than that fellow!"

Sensible Advice on Domestic Economy

"THE IMMUTABLE rule in regard to the division of family property at the time of marriage," said the experienced go-between from Kyoto, "is as follows: Let us suppose that a certain man is worth a thousand *kan*. To the eldest son at his marriage will go four hundred *kan*, together with the family residence. The second son's share will be three hundred *kan*, and he too is entitled to a house of his own. The third son will be adopted into another family, requiring a portion of one hundred *kan*. If there is a daughter, her dowry will be thirty *kan*, in addition to a bridal trousseau worth twenty *kan*. It is advisable to marry her off to the son of a family of lower financial status. Formerly it was not unusual to spend forty *kan* on the trousseau and allot ten *kan* for the dowry, but because people today are more interested in cash, it is now customary to give the daughter silver in the lacquered chest and copper in the extra one. Even if the girl is so ugly that she can't afford to sit near the candle at night, that dowry of thirty *kan* will make her bloom into a very flowery bride!

"But be that as it may,"[1] continued the voice of experience, "there is certainly more to be said. Keep in mind that she is the spoiled darling of rich parents, accustomed to being fed on the choicest viands and daintiest morsels. Her round face with protruding cheekbones is really not so bad to look at after all. That bulging forehead, of course, will enable her to wear a veiled headdress more gracefully. Her wide-set nostrils are but a guarantee that she will never be short of breath. Her sparse hair will make it cool for her in summer. Her ample waistline will prove to be no drawback if she will only cover it with a magnificent over-garment. Her fat fingers will enable her to grasp all the more firmly the neck of the midwife."

In this manner, the man took one flaw after another and recast it as an asset. "In matchmaking, money is a very important consideration," he continued. "If thirty *kan* of silver is deposited with a trustworthy merchant at six-tenths per cent interest per month, the income will total one hundred and eighty *monme* monthly, which will more than suffice to support four women: the bride, her personal maid, a second maid, and a seamstress. How unselfish must be the disposition of a bride who will not only look after the household faithfully, meantime taking care never to displease her husband's family, but also at the same time will actually pay for the food she eats! If you are looking merely for beauty, then go where women are made up solely to that end, to the licensed quar-

---

[1] *SNKBZ* punctuates this phrase as the beginning of the go-between's monologue, attributing, by default, the preceding lines to the narrator. In the original the go-between is not mentioned until long after his monologue has begun; the initial attribution has been placed earlier in this translation for the sake of clarity.

ters. You are free to visit them any time of night you may wish, and thoroughly enjoy it, but next morning you will have to pay out seventy-one *monme*, which is not in the least enjoyable!

"A more thorough investigation will reveal the fact that the saké served at a house of assignation amounts to four *bu*, while in a male brothel the rice cooked in tea consumed will cost eight *bu*. When you actually come to think of it," continued the man of experience, "you will realize that though the cost is exorbitant it is but inevitable, for as with 'Baking pans of double price,' a margin to protect against loss must be added to the selling price. Not infrequently a customer will run up a huge bill then run out on it, in utter and base disregard for all sense of love and duty. Since it is impossible for the master to collect the money from him, his name will be crossed off his account book and the rascal himself given up as dead. Whereupon the master will solemnly strike the brazier with the fire tongs and utter a fearsome imprecation: 'May you spend your next existence as a hungry ghost! May all your baked ducks, your cedar-smoked roast fish, and every other delicacy you like to order to appease your extravagant tastes, be burned to cinders, that you may be taught how terrible is the punishment for the crime of cheating on your debts!' This curse he utters with a fearsome look of resentment, quite different from the expression on his face when receiving a striped *haori* made in the province of Hida.

"It is better on the whole," continued the wise old go-between, "to give up dissipation in good time, for a roué is seldom happy in later life. So even if life at home seems dry and tasteless, you'd better have patience with a supper of cold rice, boiled tofu, and dried fish. You can always have one of your tenants repeat for you the story of Lord Itakura's gourd justice,[2] just for the fun of it. Or you may lie down whenever you like, at perfect ease, and have a maid pull your toes for you. If you want tea, you may sip it while your wife holds the cup for you. A man in his own household is the commander supreme, whose authority none will dare to question, and there is none to condemn you. There's no need to seek further for genuine pleasure.

"Then, too, there are certain business advantages to staying home. Your clerks will stop their imprudent visits to the teahouses of the Yasaka quarters and their clandestine meetings at that rendezvous in Oike. And when in the shop, since they can't appear to be completely idle, maybe they'll look over those reports from the Edo branch office, or do some other work that they have forgotten about—all to the profit of you, the master! The apprentice boys will diligently twist wastepaper into string, and in order to impress you, the master, listening in the inner rooms, they will practice penmanship to their profit, reading aloud from a copybook. Kyūshichi, whose habit it is to retire early, will take the straw packing from around the yellowtail and make rope on which to string coins; while your maid Take, in order to make things go more smoothly tomorrow, will prepare turnips for breakfast. The seamstress during the time you're at home will take off as many knots of Hino silk as she ordinarily does in a whole day. Even the cat keeps guard in the kitchen, carefully watching the cutting board and raising the alarm if she hears the least sound in the vicinity of the fish hanger. If such unmeasured profit as this results from the master's remaining at home just

---

[2] Itakura Katsushige (1545–1624) is said to have decided an inheritance case on the basis of how a gourd came to rest when placed on a surface (*SNKBZ* p. 383 note 34).

one night, think how vast will be the benefits that will accrue within the space of a whole year! So even if you are not entirely satisfied with your wife, you have to exercise discretion and realize that in the pleasure quarter all is but vanity. For a young master to be well aware of this is the secret of the successful running of his household."

Such was the counsel offered by the veteran go-between from Kyoto on New Year's Eve. Though he dwelt upon it at some length, it was advice well worth listening to.

Be that as it may, let me say that the women of today, under the influence of the styles of the pleasure quarter, dress exactly like the women employed there. Prominent drapers' wives, who in public are addressed as mesdames, are so attired as to be mistaken for licensed-quarter prostitutes; while the wives of small shopkeepers, who once served as clerks of the drapers, look exactly like the class of prostitute who works at a bathhouse. In turn, the kimono worn by wives of tailors and embroiderers who live on side streets bear a startling resemblance to those of the women employed in teahouses. It is fun to spot them in a crowd dressed in conformity with their respective degrees of fortune. A woman, after all, is only a woman: there are few, if any, marked differences between professionals and non-professionals. But by comparison the non-professionals seem slow-witted, ungainly, and unrefined in letter-writing. Neither can they drink saké in nearly so graceful a manner as the professionals. Nor can they sing songs. They wear their kimono so clumsily that they seem to hang loose about them. They move so awkwardly that when walking down the street they're unsteady on their feet. In bed they can talk of nothing but miso and salt. They're so stingy that they will only use one tissue at a time. They only think of aloeswood as a medicine, not as a scent. In any and in all respects they are disappointing, and even in their hair styles, which are copied after those of prostitutes, there is a world of difference.

Any prostitute-chaser must be an exceptionally smart fellow. Despite his cleverness, however, and his knowledge that money is hard to earn, he won't pay his debts though urgently pressed to do so—not even when he is being sued for non-payment. Yet he dares to reserve the services of his favorite courtesan for the entire New Year's holiday, in utter disregard of the cost. He will even pay in advance the whole bill as early as the thirteenth of the twelfth month, the very first day of the preparation season for the New Year. Shrewd though this fellow is about many things, he is blinded by the pleasures he finds in the licensed quarters.

A prosperous merchant of Karasuma Street, Kyoto, on retiring from business, gave to each of his two sons five hundred *kan*. The younger son steadily increased his wealth, until all his relatives believed that he was worth two thousand *kan*. As for the elder son, when New Year's Eve rolled around in the fourth year of his independence, he felt compelled to utter a fervent prayer of thanksgiving to Heaven that the night was dark. Had the moon been shining brightly, the memory of his former respectability would never have allowed him to walk the streets of Kyoto selling pepper. Under cover of darkness, with head and face concealed in a paper hood, he wandered about unnoticed, a poor peddler of pepper, till the New Year dawned upon him. The place to which his aimless feet had carried him was none other than the Tanba Highway, which was also the entrance to the Shimabara licensed quarter. Memories of better days came back to him, when he used to enter that very gate at dawn. But now he had to turn his weary footsteps homeward.

Life and Doorposts: Both are Borrowed

G ENERALLY speaking, when we get accustomed to something, it no longer worries us. At the entrance of Shimabara, the notorious licensed quarter of the capital, there is a certain stretch of rice field, through which runs the famed "Lane of Shujaka" of the popular ballad. In autumn when the rice is ripening, the farmers make a scarecrow to frighten the birds away. They set it up in the field with an old sedge hat on its head and a bamboo cane in its hand. But as the kites and crows are used to seeing the great sedge hats marked with the brands of the tea shops that lend them to pleasure-seekers wishing to hide their faces, they are no longer scared away, probably taking the scarecrow to be some unaccompanied big spender. By and by they even dare to perch on the hat, treating the straw man as just another stray man-about-town.

In this world there is surely nothing more terrible than an encounter with a bill collector. Nonetheless, when one has become accustomed over the years to being in debt, even on New

Year's Eve he will not leave the house to avoid being dunned.

A veteran debtor was proudly boasting one New Year's Eve: "Nobody has ever had his head cut off for failing to pay a debt. Not that I won't pay so long as I am able. But you can't get blood out of a turnip. How I wish I had a money tree! But sad to say there's none at hand for I never sowed the seed."

So saying he spread out an old straw mat in the sun near a tree in the corner of his garden, sat down and began polishing kitchen knives and cooking-chopsticks. "Even though I'm going to the trouble of taking the rust off this knife, now there's nothing to cut with it. Not even a single anchovy! Still it may serve some useful purpose. Human emotions are unpredictable; at any moment now I may wax so indignant that I'll kill myself. Through fifty-six years I've lived my life, but now I'm no longer attached to it. It's a pity that in Kyoto's Central Ward so many potbellied plutocrats are fated to die young. I swear by our guardian deity Lord Inari that if only one of them would pay off all my debts for me I'd gladly die in his stead by committing *hara-kiri*."

Thus speaking, he brandished his blade and looked exactly as though he were possessed by a fox.[1] At this very moment a Tōmaru rooster came by crowing. "Come," he called to it, "I'll take you along with me on my journey into the next world." With a single sweep of his sharp blade he sliced off its head.

Seeing this, the bill collectors who had been waiting about were suddenly seized with fright. Next thing they knew he'd be picking a quarrel with them on the very slightest pretext. So one after another they took their leave. On parting, however, they did not forget to speak words of consolation to the debtor's wife, who had begun to kindle a fire under the teaket-

---

[1] Foxes were (and are) thought to serve as Inari's messengers.

tle. They expressed profound sympathy that she was so unfortunate as to be the wife of so short-tempered a fellow.

To resort to such a dodge as this to be rid of bill collectors at the end of the year was nothing new; it was, however, a mean trick. Nevertheless, by this means the old reprobate was able to tide over his year-end financial embarrassment without uttering a single word of apology to anyone.

There remained, however, one young apprentice to a timber dealer in Horikawa Street who had not taken his leave with the other bill collectors. Being only eighteen or nineteen years old, though corners had been shaved into his hairline he still had his forelocks,[2] and he looked both weak and womanish, but his heart was as strong as a lion's. All the while the seasoned debt dodger had been making his threats, the young apprentice had been lingering on the bamboo veranda, unconcernedly telling the beads of his rosary, quietly chanting the prayer to Amida Buddha. When the last of the others had disappeared and the commotion had died down, he spoke up with great deliberation: "Now that the show's over, I'd like to get my bill paid and be on my way."

"What!" cried the debtor. "Even the grown-ups thought better of staying here, but there you sit and even dare to condemn my conduct as a mere act. Just what do you mean by this, anyhow?"

"At a time like this," replied the apprentice, "when we're all so busy, I consider that little act of yours to be an unnecessary trick."

---

[2] The corners shaven into a youth's hairline showed that he had entered adolescence; his forelocks would be shaven clean when he underwent a coming-of-age ceremony and officially entered adulthood. See the Introduction for a description of the sexual significance of the status of *wakashu* (youth) thus visually indicated.

"Mind your own business!" exploded the angry debtor.

"I'm not leaving here until I get..."

"Get what!" shouted the thoroughly angry fellow.

". . . get my money," calmly finished the apprentice.

"Who's going to take it?" came the angry retort.

"What do you mean 'who'?" replied the self-possessed apprentice. "I'm an expert, you know, at this sort of thing. Among all my fellow bill collectors, none would even attempt to collect from this list of twenty-seven notorious debtors. Take a look at this account book I have here. So far I've checked off the names of twenty-six and I've no intention of quitting here until I've collected your debt. Until you have paid your bill, the timbers you used to repair your house belong to us. So I'll carry them off with me."

Suiting action to words, the young apprentice forthwith took up his sledge hammer and began tearing out the doorposts of the house.

Whereupon the master of the house jumped up and rushed toward him, crying out, "You rascal! I won't stand for such an insult."

"Come, come," replied the apprentice in a mollifying tone of voice, "the style of your threat is out of date. You seem to be completely ignorant of the current fashion. To tear out doorposts is the very latest thing in effective bill collecting."

Since the young man showed no signs whatever of being frightened by his threats, there was nothing left for the old debtor to do but apologize to him and pay in full the overdue bill.

When the young apprentice had checked the last of the twenty-seven names off his list of unpaid accounts, he turned to the now thoroughly subdued debtor and said, "Now that I've been paid there's nothing further to say. However, let me tell you this much anyhow. Your entire technique of resistance is quite passé. Experienced old campaigner that you are, your style is definitely dated. It would be much better if you'd coach your wife well in advance. Start your quarrel with her about noon on New Year's Eve. Have her change her kimono, all the while crying out: 'Any moment now I'm ready to get a divorce from you. But I warn you that if it comes to this, several people will die. Do you understand this thoroughly? It's no laughing matter in the least. So you want me to leave? I guess I'll have to. I'll show you!' At this point you say to her, 'How I've yearned to pay my debts so when I die people will speak well of me, for the proverb says, "Man is mortal but fame is lasting." Much as I regret it, this has come to pass. There's nothing I can do about it. This very day will be my last on this earth. Oh, what a pity!' Lamenting after this fashion, then, you ought to grab some papers—any old worthless paper will do. Tear them into shreds one after another, just as though they were valuable documents. When they see you do this, even the most obstinate of bill collectors will feel compelled to leave the scene at once."

Having listened attentively to the advice of the young apprentice, the old debtor spoke: "That's a trick I've never tried. Now, thanks to your suggestion I'll win through the next year end." Turning to his wife he asked, "What do you think of it, my dear? Isn't it a wonder that a lad so young should show a wisdom so superior to my own? An occasion such as this calls for a celebration."

Quickly the rooster slain shortly before was converted into soup, and then, with the apprentice boy an honored guest, the two ate the dinner and drank saké to celebrate the successful end of the year.

The meal done and the boy gone, the old veteran had second thoughts: "It's not just the next year end that we must watch," he cogitated. "Those persistent bill collectors will be assaulting us again before the new year dawns." Immediately he began mapping out with his wife the strategy they would employ in their rehearsed quarrels.

So competently did he manage to deal with the bill collectors by means of his newly acquired technique that thereafter his fame spread abroad as the "Quarreler of Ōmiya Street."

The Opening
Performance by the
New Players

IN THE THEATERS of Kyoto it is customary to perform as a prelude to the opening of performances around the time of the New Year a dance to congratulate the city on its prosperity. Indeed, the thriving townspeople of Kyoto, who benefit from direct rule by the shogun, are as generous as generous can be when occasion demands, which is due entirely to their never-ending figuring and the economy-minded living of their lives day by day.

In the autumn of last year, the nō master Takeda Gonbei of the Konparu school troupe sponsored by the Kaga domain held a performance in Kyoto for which the public was charged admission. The price of theater boxes for the four-day spectacle was set at ten pieces of silver, but they were soon sold out. Furthermore, cash in advance was paid for them.

At first it was announced that the tragic drama *Sekidera Komachi* would be presented, and people were greatly excited in expectation of seeing this play as it was to be performed according to a secretly transmitted technique. But when the hand drummer, for some reason or other, found it impossible to perform his part, the program was changed. Despite the alteration, however, on the opening day even before dawn, people thronged the entrance to the theater. Among them was a man from Edo who had reserved two entire boxes, each of which had cost him ten pieces of silver. In one of them he spread out a crimson rug, and further equipped it with a portable shelf, a low folding screen, and a case for his personal effects. In the back of the box he set up a temporary kitchen, provided with fish, fowl, and a basket of seasonal fruit. In the other box he set up a teakettle, with two cedar pails of water beside it for making tea, one labeled "Uji Bridge" and the other "Otowa River."

Seated with him in his boxes were to be seen a physician, a draper, a Confucian scholar, a dealer in imported goods, and a linked-verse poetry master; while visible behind them were the owners of, respectively, a house of assignation in the Shimabara prostitution quarter and a male brothel in Shijō employing young kabuki actors, a brothel-quarter entertainer well known in the city, a masseur, and a ronin known for his swordsmanship. Under the boxes was space for his personal palanquin, a bath, and even a lavatory. Indeed, with such luxurious appointments nothing at all was lacking in convenience for the enjoyment of the play.

Such was the magnanimity of this man from Edo. Yet he was not the son of a daimyo; he had attained to his position of eminence solely by dint of his wealth. Which is a very good reason why you should make money above all things else, in order that you too might disport yourself as you please. But there was method in this man's madness about the theater, for he was very careful in all his entertaining to see that his wealth suffered no impairment. When business is combined with pleasure, how enjoyable it is!

If a man is not rich enough, however, he should under no circumstances spend money wastefully around the time of the first frost. When the festival held on the ninth day of the ninth month is past, it seems to be the usual custom for people to relax their attention to business, for then the year end still seems to be a thing of the distant future. With the coming of the tenth month, however, the weather changes: it becomes unsettled, and the rain and the winds threaten. In such an atmosphere as this it seems only natural for people to become nervous and restless. They tend to postpone until the New Year any particular thing they may have been planning, and they make shift with the bare necessities of daily life. Under such conditions they give up any ideas they might have had about buying luxuries or the works of artisans. By and by, when the morning frost and the evening blasts drive them early to bed and near to the *kotatsu* provided for their comfort during winter's confinement, they are again liable to neglect their business, and as a result they may come to the end of the year hard pressed.

Later on there will follow, one after the other, the death anniversary of Nichiren, founder of the Buddhist sect that takes his name, the series of ten evening services by the Jōdo sect, the death anniversary of the founder of the Tōfukuji Temple, as well as observances for that of the founder of the Ikkō sect. The daytime festival and the evening merrymaking for the Day of the Boar come close together, only to be followed shortly by the bonfire ceremony at shrines to the god Inari.

Likewise about this time of year, the members of the kabuki troupes of the dry riverbed at Shijō are changed, and the first performances of the new troupes are staged. Actors of long-standing reputation seem fresh again, and a mood of excitement overtakes the viewing public. One day they're gossiping about a certain troupe leader and the next day about another, then the following day they're talking about a young actor from Osaka who will be appearing at yet another theater. And through the teahouse attached to the theater they reserve box seats and give generous tips to actors they've gotten to know backstage, so that they might be hailed as their "patrons"—a very hollow and useless vanity indeed!

Drunk with the saké they have brought into the theater, they do not return straight home after the performance, but linger to watch the epilogue dance again in the upstairs room in Ishigake Street. So boisterously do they talk and so uproariously do they carouse that one would fear they could be heard all the way to the top of Mt. Hiei. As these carousers are prominent people in Kyoto, however, other people talk about them: "Oh, yes! He's the favorite draper of Mr. So-and-So," or, "He's the broker that has entrée to Lord What-You-May-Call-'im's house." To be thus gossiped about is considered by these habitués of the amusement districts to be an honor.

However, in the case of a merchant with little capital, the story is entirely different. If he attends the theater just to beguile the time, he must be careful not to sit next to a smoker, lest the craving to smoke overcome him; and as for a cushion for his seat—well, he had better rent one made of straw. Still, from where he sits he can learn the names of the actors just as easily as anybody else.

Now on the very opening day, when Yojibei and his troupe staged their new program, several young men who looked as if they cared not a straw whether or not they were disinherited, were seen to be seated in the second box to the left of the stage. Being fashionably dressed, they were sent amorous glances by the boy actors on the stage, to the great envy of all the spectators sitting below them in the pit. Seated in the audience, however, was one man who happened to have inside information about them, and he revealed their stories as follows:

"Though I don't know exactly how rich or how poor they are, I do know this: they are people from the River West section of the city. Isn't it amusing to see them putting on as grand airs as the people of the Central Ward? Why, a stranger might mistake them for men of distinction. That fellow dressed in the black *haori* married the heiress of a rice dealer strictly from mercenary motives, taking on her family's name and being adopted by his in-laws. His wife must be fourteen or fifteen years older than he is. He makes the mother of his bride operate the treadle of a rice-polisher that holds two *shō* of grain, and he sets his younger brother to tramping about the streets of Kyoto selling broad beans. He ought to quit wearing that white-hilted sword.

"That fellow wearing the iridescent *haori* is a glue dealer of uncertain origin, though from his flashy clothes you might suppose he was more respectable than he is. His house is mortgaged and he is being sued for not keeping up with the payments on it. Besides, he has a dispute over the eastern boundary line with his neighbor that, because of his obstinacy, has not been settled yet. At such a critical time as this, it is sheer madness for him to show up in the theater.

"That third fellow over there in the light-brown *haori* is known to have borrowed five *kan*—not without paying interest, of course—for a dowry that would enable him to marry into a lacquerer's family and become adopted by them. His foster father hasn't been dead thirty-five days, yet here he sits in the theater, leaving his poor widowed mother alone at home.

What an uncouth fellow he is! At a time when no merchant in Kyoto is willing to sell him rice, or fuel, or any other daily necessity on credit, he calls in prostituted young kabuki actors to drink with him. Poor lads, they think he's a rich patron, because it's humanly impossible for them to find out the truth about him. Quite contrary to their belief, though, he hasn't paid for any credit purchases for the past four or five years.

"That fellow wearing the *haori* with a printed stripe pattern runs a small money-changing shop. His brother is a priest in Miidera Temple, and with his assistance he'll be able to scrape past the year end. Except for him, probably not a single one of them will be able to stay in the capital to celebrate the New Year."

As he spoke, he pointed in their direction and laughed; whereupon, misinterpreting it as an expression of envy, they took two or three kumquats, and, placing them on a bed of camellia leaves and daffodils, wrapped them up in tissue paper and tossed them over in his direction.

Opening up the package, our narrator smiled in derision and remarked, "If they were the big spenders that they pretend to be, they would have paid two *bu* for every single kumquat. But you may be sure they'll never pay for them at all."

By and by the entire program ended and our running commentator took his leave and went home. Thereafter the same crowd appeared in the theater district day after day, but always dressed in the same kimono and wearing the identical *haori*. When the manager of a teahouse employing prostitutes noticed it; he at once asked them to pay their bills. But they declined to do so, and after that they abruptly ceased coming to the theater district.

Soon it was New Year's Eve and one of them, judging it old-fashioned to skip out on his bills at night, ran off in broad daylight to points unknown. Another was confined to his room on the pretext of being insane. Still another, who tried to commit suicide, was thereafter kept under observation. As for the brothel-quarter entertainer who had introduced these fellows to the teahouse, he was put under police surveillance for having endorsed thieves.

The teahouse keeper, who could think of nothing to do but despair of ever collecting his money, finally managed to persuade himself that it was all a horrible nightmare and beat a hasty retreat. Whereas he had anticipated earning fifteen *ryō* from them, all that remained with him after the episode were three sedge hats left behind and the rather painful proof that on New Year's Eve he was the biggest dupe in Kyoto.

How Lovely the Sight
of Rice-Cake Flowers
at New Year's

"**B**E QUICK to do good," the proverb says, and sure enough, bill collectors move fast when making their rounds on the last day of the year. They race about with the speed of the guardian deity Idaten, such that even if their straw sandals were made of iron they would wear them out on this special day. As for merchants, the energy that they apply to their businesses determines whether they win or lose the race.

A skilled bill collector with several years of experience once said, "To be successful in collecting bills you must start with the one who pays most readily and then work up to the hard one who is notorious for nonpayment. Be careful not to trip over your own tongue. If the debtor behaves in a manner calculated to irritate you, remain all the calmer and speak only of the matter at hand, and that with a persuasive tongue. Sit down on the threshold in a leisurely manner, tell your porter to put out the light, and talk in a way similar to this:

"'What crime did I commit in a former life that I should have been condemned to suffer in this one as a bill collector? I have yet to celebrate New Year's Day even once with my pate properly shaven. My wife has to work for my financial backer as human collateral and has to try to please even his clerks. Of all the hundreds of possible ways to earn a living, why should I ever have chosen such a mode of life as this? Sometimes I feel like reproaching the tutelary god of my birthplace, even though I know he hasn't anything to do with my present sorry lot.

"'In contrast, though I'm a stranger to your household affairs, I'm sure the mistress lacks nothing to make her as blissful as a Buddha. Those lovely rice-cake flowers hanging from the ceiling are full of the rejoicing of the New Year season. And by the way, whenever I go to someone's house the fish hanger is the first thing I notice. Oh, just look at the duck, and the dried sea cucumbers, and the skewered abalone hanging there on yours. I'm sure you've already had a kimono made to wear for the New Year's holiday. The crests in vogue now with the ladies are a peony flower with leaves, and four ginkgo leaves combined in a circle. I wish my wife could afford to wear fashionable and up-to-date kimono. It's so true that clothes make the woman. Say, Omatsu! I'll bet that the kimono the master gave you has a medium-sized, stylized paulownia blossom pattern against a dark brown background. You are lucky to be working in this house. Out on the edge of town I see many women wearing kimono featuring old-fashioned arabesque designs.'

"In this manner you will both buy time and try to induce the wife to say something. Then, when the other bill collectors are not around, the master of the house will quietly come to you and say that although he is determined not to pay anybody else this year end, because you have opened up to him about your own situation he'll pay you this much, even though it's the money he's saved up for his wife's pilgrimage to the Grand Shrine at Ise. The balance he will pay you before the third month, when he hopes to see your smiling face again.

"So saying, he will pay you sixty *monme* out of a hundred due. In olden times they used to pay eighty *monme* out of a hundred. Twenty years ago they would have paid half the debt without fail. Ten years ago a forty-percent payment was prevalent, but nowadays they will pay only thirty *monme* out of a hundred, which usually includes at least two bad pieces of silver. Thus people's hearts grow more and more debased, and such is the situation existing between creditor and debtor. What a nuisance to the creditor! But for him there is no escape from it unless he goes out of business, which he cannot afford to do. Whereupon, forgetting the troubles of the year end he will again start selling to customers on credit.

"It is fascinating how customs change with the times. In olden times the creditor accepted the debtor's excuse for failure to pay up, and after midnight on New Year's Eve stopped trying to collect bills overdue. Later, when collectors persevered until dawn, quarrels broke out wherever they went. Quite recently, although collections are made far into the wee hours of the morning, no angry words arise between creditor and debtor, for all is settled without too much fuss.

"Just how is it settled that way? 'The truth is that where there's no money, there's just no money to be got,' declares the debtor, not afraid to be overheard by his neighbors. 'In this floating world even daimyo are in debt! No one's been beheaded yet for failure to pay his debts, even though they may amount to a thousand *kan*. If I really had any money to pay, I wouldn't put you off. Oh, how I wish this cauldron were filled with one-*bu* silver pieces! Then I could clear off all my debts at once. Actually, money is the most biased thing I know; it actually seems to hate me.'

"So speaking, he will then break into a chant from a nō play, intoning, 'Now you are up, then you are down. That's the way of the world.' Meantime, while stretched at full length on the floor, he beats time on his wooden pillow like a hand drum.

"That sort of fellow is simply beyond me! Since he defies all sense of shame and decency, the average bill collector figures it will simply be a waste of time to talk with him any further; so he strikes off his old credits and discounts the new ones. Thus the two reach an amicable compromise instead of continuing to quarrel. Today people have grown wiser."

When you consider carefully the state of the world, you will realize that it is better to have a foolish son than a smart clerk, for the son is by nature honest. When he sets out to collect bills he never does the job halfheartedly, for he knows that the money will be his own someday. On the other hand, the young employee with sincere regard for his master, who attends to his duties faithfully, understands his position and has good sense is rather an exception, for rare indeed is the employee who is devoted to his master's interests. He would prefer to visit the pleasure quarter, where each day a thousand pieces of gold are squandered. If he collects a payment in full, he pilfers some of the money, entering it in his notebook as "short." Or he may surreptitiously exchange good gold for bad, or exchange silver for copper and misappropriate the financial profit gained thereby to his own personal uses. Those credits of which the master is ignorant he may possibly enter as "non-collectable." Even the shrewdest master cannot keep up with all the varied forms of embezzlement.

In the case of a petty merchant's apprentice, he too fails to pay sincere attention to his bill collecting. Instead, he buys a deck of cards at the Hoteiya shop, puts marks on the backs of them and walks along the street trying to memorize these, at a time when he ought to be busy working. Anyway, his actions are of no profit to his master.

Bill collectors are not all of the same character, but few are good people. Hence it is of great importance to be on guard all day long, considering every man to be a robber, just as truly as fire is caused by the careless handling of fuel.

Once there lived a certain Chūroku, a talkative man whom others nicknamed "Furuna" after the Buddha's most eloquent disciple. He worked as a construction foreman, and since he was forever cracking jokes he gained the reputation of being the town's chief unofficial entertainer. His mimicry unfailingly pleased when people gathered at night to await the rising of the moon or sun.[1] Well, when the eve of the current year approached, he found that he would be hard pressed to tide over the year end. So he went to the home of one of his patrons and asked him for a loan of five hundred *monme* of silver. His request being quickly granted, he was so delighted that he returned after dark to his patron's house, sat formally at the entrance to the kitchen and intoned his best wishes for the New Year in the following verses:

SONG OF CHŪROKU ON NEW YEAR'S EVE
How merry the notes of the koto
That fall this eve on my ears!
Hearing it one feels
He's in the house of an ageless immortal.

---

[1] Such gatherings, which were both social and religious in nature, were held at particular points in the lunar calendar.

In all the wide city of Osaka,
There's no other house: far or near,
That with silver and gold is surrounded,
With treasures beyond compare,

With the cloak that makes you invisible,
And the hat that makes you the same.
Oh, the mallet that makes your money scales ring[2]
Is Daikoku's hammer of fortune and fame.

How blest is my master!

On hearing this the master entered and said, "Chūroku, you seem to be waiting to see me. Is it for this?" So saying, he tossed him five hundred *monme* wrapped up in a sheet of paper. Chūroku raised it to his forehead thrice, each time repeating appropriate expressions of gratitude. "Thanks to you," he said with feeling, "I shall now be able to tide over the year end.

I'll take my leave now, for before long the cock will be crowing." When he got as far as the doorway, he trotted back to ask the maids to tell the mistress how grateful he was. Whereupon one of them, a mid-ranking maidservant named Kichi, reminded him that this was a most auspicious season. "You 're right!" he said gaily, "Perhaps I should do a dance."

While Chūroku was engaged in such prolonged felicitation, the head clerk of the household suddenly returned from business in the northern provinces and as he entered the house he cried out, "We must send two hundred *kan* to the warehouse office at once. The rice will be arriving any minute, and we stand to make a lot of money from it. Cash, cash! We

---

[2] A small wooden mallet used to adjust the scales.

are badly in need of cash. This is not the time for singing and playing the koto, even for you women. Somehow we'll have to raise that cash."

At this moment his eye happened to light on the five hundred *monme* which Chūroku had left on the threshold. He snatched it up, crying, "Oh, what a lot of money we have here! How dare anyone leave it lying around so carelessly? Two hundred *kan* in cash is the money we need. Let's see whether or not we have that much in the house. If not, we'll have to send out search parties to scour the city until we raise it. O money, money, money! My kingdom for some money!"

The clerk had created such a furor that poor Chūroku was completely nonplussed. So he apologized for having stayed so long and with empty hands beat a hasty retreat.

Golden Dreams

"**D**ON'T forget your business," admonished a millionaire, "even in your dreams." For in your sleep you are sure to dream of what gives you most concern. Sometimes the dreams are happy, sometimes they are sad. But there's something contemptible about dreaming of finding money by the roadside. In any case, nowadays no one would ever lose his pocketbook, for he cares as much for it as he does for his life. No, you couldn't find a single *mon* in the vicinity of a temple where the Ten-Thousand-Day Service[1] has just been held, nor even on the very next day after the Tenma Festival. The fact is that money won't come to you unless you work for it.

There was a certain poor fellow of Fushimi who longed to become rich all at one jump, although he habitually neglected his work day by day. He had formerly lived in Edo, where in

---

[1] During which a single day's visit to the temple was supposed to accrue the same amount of merit as ten thousand days of visits.

those days loose silver could be seen piled up in the money exchange shops in Suruga-chō. Such a vivid impression had it made upon his mind that he still recalled the sight.

"Oh, how I wish I owned such a heap of silver at this year end!" he sighed to himself. "There was also a heap of newly minted gold *koban* that took up as much space as I would have if I had lain down on the deerskin where they were piled up," and he lay back on his paper-covered futon, obsessed with his thoughts of money.

It was the night before the last day of the year, and the following morning his wife awoke at dawn while he continued to sleep. "I don't know how we'll make it through the day," she thought, worrying about their household finances. Then, glancing in the direction of a sunbeam that had just come peeping in through the eastern window, she saw, to her great amazement, a heap of gold. "Oh, my goodness!" she cried aloud, awakening her husband. "This is literally a gift from heaven!"

"What's the matter?" he asked drowsily. But at that very instant, much to her great disappointment the gold disappeared. When she told him what she had seen, her husband remarked, "The temporary manifestation of gold to you must have been caused by my attachment to all that money I saw when we were living in Edo. My situation is so hopeless at present that I would gladly toll the bell of damnation at Nakayama in Sayo. I wish I could be saved from poverty in this present world, even though it might mean damnation for me in the next. Why, in this present life rich people enjoy a veritable paradise, while we poor people suffer the very tortures of hell. We have absolutely nothing! Not even a stick of firewood to burn under a cooking pot. Oh, what a miserable way to end the year!"

Even as such wicked desires arose in his mind, his soul was changed from good to evil. When he fell into a doze, he dreamed of the black and white messengers of hell, drawing a rumbling fiery cart behind them, and pointing out to him the boundary line between his world and theirs. When he awoke and told his wife of the dream, she grew all the sadder and thus admonished him:

"No one can live to be a hundred. So it is unwise of you to entertain such a silly desire. In future, if our love for each other does not diminish a bit but remains constant, we can hope to celebrate New Year's Day happily. I can well imagine how it must vex you sometimes when you think what I have to put up with. But if things continue as bad as they are now, the three of us will starve to death.

"It's fortunate for us that I now have an offer of employment. It will also be a good thing for the future of our only child. If you will be so kind as to bring her up with your own hand, we may still look forward to happiness at some future time. It would be cruel to abandon her, so I'm begging you to keep her with you." All the while she spoke she was choking with tears, which so overwhelmed her husband with grief that he could say not a word in reply, but shut his eyes against the tears, unable to look her in the face.

Just then a woman employment agent from the Sumizome district arrived at the house, in company with an old woman some sixty years old. "As I was telling you yesterday," she said to the young mother, "you have good breasts; so you will be paid eighty-five *monme* in advance, and in addition you may have new kimono made for you four times a year. You ought to be grateful for such generous treatment. Why, the pay of a kitchen maid so tall she reaches the clouds[2] who does the weaving in addition to her regular work is only thirty-two *monme* every six months. It's because of your milk, you know, that you are being paid so well. If you turn down this offer, I have another candidate for the job in the northern part of Kyōmachi Street. Anyway," she concluded, "since we must have a wet nurse beginning today, you'll have to make up your mind."

Speaking in a spirit of self-sacrifice the wife replied, "It's only because we don't want to starve. Now my chief concern is whether or not I'll be able to do my duty successfully to the beloved son of my new master. In any case, I sincerely desire to work for him."

"Then let's start as soon as possible," replied the agent, completely ignoring the husband. She then borrowed a brush and ink from the next-door neighbor, wrote out a contract for a year, and handed her the sum of money in cash. At the same time, however, she shrewdly kept back her commission of eight and a half *monme* out of the money envelope on which was written "Eighty-five *monme*; thirty-seven pieces." "It's all the same whether I take it out now or later," she said defensively. "Anyhow, this is what everybody does."

"And now, my dear nurse," continued the agent, "there's no need to stop to change clothes." And she started to leave at once. The husband was dissolved in tears. The wife, also flushed with weeping, spoke to her baby, saying, "Goodbye, Oman. Mama is now leaving to go to her new master's home, but some day during the first month of the New Year[3] she will

---

[2] Tall female servants were paid more (*SNKBZ* p. 411 note 14).

[3] The sixteenth of the first month was a holiday for servants (*SNKBZ* p. 412 note 11).

come back to see you." She then asked her neighbors to take good care of her baby, and once again burst into tears.

Altogether unmoved by what she witnessed, the woman business agent hardheartedly declared, "Babies can grow up without parents. If one is not going to die, he won't die even if you beat him to death. So long, mister!"

And so saying, she walked away. However, the old woman who had come along with her was moved with compassion. She looked back toward the poor husband and baby and sighed, "Just as I felt sorry for my dear grandson when he lost his mother, it's a pity to see someone else's baby taken from her mother's breast." The agent, with no regard for the feelings of the mother who stood beside her, called back to the old woman, "It can't be helped, for money runs this world. It's really no concern of ours whether that girl lives or dies." And so saying, and stonyhearted as ever, she hurried away with the mother.

Meantime the evening came on, the eve of New Year's Day. The poor fellow, now acutely aware of the impermanence of all things, mumbled to himself, "I inherited a considerable fortune, but because of my bad management I lost it all and had to leave Edo. It was due solely to my wife's considerate efforts that I was able to settle down here in Fushimi. Even if we should have nothing but 'good-luck tea' to toast the parting year, we could still be happy if only we could celebrate New Year's Day together. Oh, what a shame!"

In expectation of eating *zōni* with his wife on New Year's Day the man had bought two pairs of chopsticks. When his glance happened to fall on them lying on a corner of the shelf he picked one up and said, "One pair is unnecessary now," and so saying he broke the chopsticks in two and threw the pieces into the kitchen fire.

When night fell, the baby began to cry and would not be comforted. The wives of the neighbors came in and showed him how to put *jiō*[4] syrup in the rice paste and water, and how to warm it up and feed it to the baby through a bamboo tube. "It may just be my imagination," remarked one of the women, "but it seems to me by the looks of her chin that this baby has lost flesh even in a single day."

"I couldn't help it," thought the man to himself. And then all of a sudden, feeling very angry with no one in particular, he hurled the fire tongs he held in his hand out into the garden. Seeing him in such agony, the wives said to one another, "Here sits a poor unhappy husband, while his wife is enjoying herself. Her new master likes to have a good-looking maid around the house, especially since she looks so much like his wife who died recently. Why, if you saw her from the back, you'd say she looks just as attractive as his dead wife did."

That did it!

No sooner had the husband heard this remark than he snatched up the money from where it had been lying untouched ever since his wife had left home, and rushed out of the house. For now he felt that he would rather die of starvation than be separated from her a moment longer.

So he brought his wife back home, and they celebrated the arrival of the New Year, in tears—but together!

---

[4] *Rehmannia glutinosa.*

Even Gods Make Mistakes Sometimes

ANNUALLY in the tenth month all the gods from each province in Japan meet at the Grand Shrine of Izumo to discuss the peace and welfare of the people. At that time also the year gods are assigned to their appointed places to speed preparations for the coming New Year. The foremost in virtue, to be sure, are chosen to look after Kyoto, Edo, and Osaka. Veteran gods are likewise assigned to Nara and Sakai; while appropriate gods are designated for Nagasaki, Ōtsu, and Fushimi. Other suitable gods are selected for appointment to castle towns where provincial lords reside, to seaports, and to the chief inland towns and mountain villages. It is the task of the gods, besides, to see that the New Year comes to even the lowliest who live in the most distant isles or the poorest huts: to each and every one, in fact, who makes up ricecakes and sets out pine branches before his doorway.

Now so far as preference goes, the gods themselves would much rather be the year gods of Kyoto and the surrounding region, for they dislike having to preside over the New Year festivities in rural areas. In any case, when a choice is given between town and country, it goes without saying that in every respect the former is preferable.

Time flows by as swiftly as the current of a stream, and all too soon comes the last day of the twelfth month. In the city of Sakai people are careful of their fortunes, always figuring out ways to protect them. Everyone puts on an appearance of living more simply than he actually does. From the outside his house is latticed in front, like that of a retired merchant, but inside it is wide and spacious. He never fails to estimate his annual income, and to live within it.

Suppose a man has a daughter. After she is over the smallpox, he gauges how beautiful or ugly she is, and if he thinks that she will possess the sort of looks that people find attractive these days, even though she is but three or maybe five years old, he will start accumulating her trousseau, piece by piece and year after year. If the daughter happens to be plain in appearance, he knows that no young man will marry her without a dowry. Therefore in addition to his regular line of business he loans out money on interest, in order to earn some extra money against the time of her marriage. This shows the sort of perspicacious fellow he is.

As a result of his foresightedness, room after room is added to his house, and before the roof becomes too old he has it reshingled. He also reinforces the beams with stone foundations before they rot away. He likewise keeps an eye on the copper gutters, and several years before he is forced to repair them, he begins a wary watch on the ups and downs of the copper market, and when the price of copper is at the bottom he has his gutters repaired. The suit of hand-woven pongee that he wears every day will not become threadbare because he never moves about hastily. His clothes, therefore, give him the appearance of a gentleman, and yet at the same time they are quite economical. He is possessed of many household things that have been handed down from one generation to the next, so when he sets out to give a year end tea, publicly he gives the impression of living a life of luxury, yet actually it doesn't cost him very much. Such are the practices of one who has managed to live in the world for a good many years.

If even rich men must practice economy, how much more essential is it for those who are not very rich. Instead of sleeping on a pillow at night he ought to rest his head on an abacus, aware even in his sleep that the approaching year end may either make him or break him. If he would like to view red maple leaves in the fall, he ought to make good use of his imagination which will enable him to see them in the cheap red rice he pounds in his hand mortar. Instead of himself eating red porgy at cherry-blossom time, he might be better advised to send it to Kyoto, where the demand for it is so great. Nay, he ought never to buy even a river carp, giving as an excuse that it smells of mud, except, of course, when he has a guest to entertain. Kyoto is surrounded by mountains, yet the people who live there eat bonito, while the people in Sakai, who live so near the sea, are content to eat smaller fish.

Indeed, as the proverb goes, "It is darkest at the foot of the lighthouse," and things are not always what they seem. One New Year's Eve, the assigned year god entered the home of a certain prosperous-looking merchant unannounced, to receive honors in celebration of the New Year, for such is the prerogative of all the year gods. In this house the New Year shelf was prepared, but there was no offertory light burning on it. There was an ominous and deserted air about the place. Nevertheless, since it was the house of his choice, and moreover, as it was inadvisable to share the entertainment with another god, which would be more than likely if he moved to another house, he remained where he was, rather curious to see just how the master would celebrate the New Year.

Now every time the door was opened, he could hear the mistress timidly repeating the same apology that her husband had not yet come home and that she was sorry the caller had come in vain so often. In the meantime midnight came and went and the dawn drew near. But still the bill collectors continued to arrive at the house one after another and began to bellow: "How soon will the master be back?" Whereupon the clerk came rushing up out of breath and reported thus: "As we were hurrying along through the middle of Sukematsu, four or five rogues of towering height suddenly fell upon us and carried the master off into a pine grove, and began to threaten him to choose between his money and his life. I barely managed to escape from them."

"You, coward!" the mistress exclaimed, appearing to be greatly astonished. "Shame upon your manhood for forsaking your master in his hour of peril when his life was at stake." Seeing her dissolved in tears, the bill collectors left the place one by one. By and by the sky began to grow brighter. When the last bill collector had disappeared, the sadness of the mistress, strangely enough, appeared to do the same. Then the clerk took out a bag of money and said to her, "The country people are pinched for money too; I was able to collect only thirty-five *monme* of silver and six hundred *zeni*." This clerk, employed in an artful and contriving household, was himself no slouch when it came to money matters.

All the while, the master had been lying well hidden in a corner of a back room, reading a tale of karmic retribution over and over again. It told of a poor ronin who lived at Fuwa, in Mino Province. The part where the ronin, finding it impossible to tide over the year end, had in desperation stabbed his wife and his child made him particularly sad. It deeply touched the master, because he saw himself in a similar plight.

"Well, he had every reason for his desperate deed," he said to himself, and fell to weeping in secret.

But when at last he was informed that all the bill collectors had given up the pursuit and gone off, he recovered his composure sufficiently to emerge timidly from his place of concealment. Complaining with a sigh that he had aged several years during the ordeal of that single night, and vainly regretting his past carelessness, he went about the task of buying rice and fuel at a time when everyone else was eating *zōni* and celebrating the season.

On New Year's Day he and his family ate ordinary rice, and it was not until the morning of the second day that they could prepare *zōni* to serve to the god and the Buddha. "For some ten years," he said apologetically, "it has been our family custom to celebrate the New Year on the *second* day. Please forgive us for using such an old tray in serving you." More than that: no food offering was made in the evening. The year god had never dreamed that the master of this house was so poor. No sooner had the first three days of the New Year gone by, than he left the house and visited Ebisu's Shrine at Imamiya, to report to him what miserable entertainment he had received at the poor man's house, a house which so utterly belied its showy external appearance.

"It was rather stupid of you, a veteran year god, not to have known better," remarked Ebisu to him. "Before you call at a house you should investigate the financial status of the master. Never enter a house whose doorway is dirty, or whose mat borders are frayed, or where the mistress has to please the maid, for they won't have the money to celebrate the New

Year properly. Although Sakai is a large city, the number of poor fellows such as the one you have told me of is really only four or five at the most. It was unlucky of you to have happened to visit one of these few. I have plenty of saké and porgy here that merchants from all the provinces have dedicated to me; so stay and eat and drink before you return to Izumo. It will take away the aftertaste of your coarse fare." So Ebisu entertained the poor year god with food and drink and let him stay awhile with him.

The foregoing story became known to mortals only because a man who visited the shrine early in the morning of Ebisu's Day happened to hear the gods talking together in the inner sanctuary. It all goes to show that even in the society of the gods there are distinctions between rich and poor. Such being the case, how natural it is that human fortunes should be so disparate in this floating world. It behooves you, therefore, to busy yourself with your regular occupation, working with all diligence, in order that the year god, who comes to you but once a year, may suffer no discomfort or inconvenience.

The Night of Insults

ACH locality has its own peculiar customs. In the Kantō districts there are some villages in which the festival for the god of a local shrine is observed on New Year's Eve. Likewise on that day, in the province of Settsu, patrons of Nishinomiya Shrine have a custom of staying at home all day long; while at Mekari Shrine in the province of Buzen on the same day they hold a divine service of seaweed gathering. In the mountain recesses of Tanba province weddings are customarily held on New Year's Eve.

The festival of the dead used to be held on New Year's Eve, so that while people busied themselves with preparations for the New Year, they had at the same time to arrange incense and flowers to place before the Buddha image. They needed to prepare both offerings to the year god and hemp-stalk chopsticks for ceremonies honoring the dead. To make things less hectic, some wise men of those days, without giving advance notice to Paradise, moved the festival of the dead to the fourteenth of the seventh month. Wise men today would prefer to hold this festival at the same time as either the spring or autumn equinox festival, which would prove to be an inestimable economical boon to uncounted future generations.

The festival of the Ikukunitama Shrine in Osaka is set for the ninth of the ninth month. Fortunately, as it is also the day of the Double-Yang Festival, on this very day each household prepares a meal of vinegared and broiled fish. Since the celebration is the same in each household, there is no danger that guests will drop in unannounced. Just figure the savings for this one occasion alone and you will discover that it mounts up to an enormous total. In this case it appears that it was out of consideration for his devotees' purses that the god fixed this day to celebrate.

Every New Year's Eve in Kyoto, at Gion Shrine[1] a service known as the Kezurikake[2] is held. First the sacred lights are dimmed until the faces of visitors are unrecognizable in the darkness. Next they divide the company into two groups, who then proceed to exchange insults, each side heaping as gross abuses as possible upon the other, much to the merriment of all the participants. For example:

"On one of the first three days of the New Year a rice cake will stick in your throat, and you'll be cremated at Toribeno."

"You are a partner in crime with a slave trader: both of you'll ride bareback to Awataguchi for your execution."

"On New Year's Day your wife will go crazy and throw your baby down the well."

"Messengers of Hell will carry you off in their fiery cart and eat you up."

"Your father was a town watchman."

---

[1] Now known as Yasaka Shrine.
[2] The name refers to the "half-shaven" wood burnt during the service.

"Your mother used to be the concubine of a Buddhist priest."

"Your little brother's a swindler's assistant."

"Your aunt's an abortionist."

"Your big sister will go out to buy miso without wearing her slip and tumble head over heels in the street."

Thus do they glibly fling coarse insults at one another, there being no limit to the catalog of abuses.

Now one of the outstanding participants in such a battle of abuse was a young man about twenty-seven or twenty-eight years old whose insults surpassed in coarseness and glibness all the rest. One opponent after another went down before his eloquent charges, until before long none would dare to challenge him. Just then there cut through the darkness from under a pine tree to the left a voice which called out: "Hey! Big boy, you talk just like you had a new outfit of clothes for the New Year. What have you got on under that kimono? On a cold night like this I bet it isn't even padded!"

It was a random shot, but it struck home. The fellow was so sorely hit in a sensitive spot that he could answer not a word, but immediately lost himself in the crowd, amidst general laughter. It seems apparent from such an incident as this that nothing hurts like the truth. Anyhow, while it is still light, you'd better start making preparations for the dark of New Year's Eve, for as the proverb runs, "Poverty is a stranger to diligence."

One evening several people were walking along Sanjō Street, none too cheerfully talking together: "Where in the world has all the gold and silver gone that's flown from this flowery capital?" asked one. "I wonder if the devils have been carrying it off with them every year when they are chased out at bean-throwing time? It seems to me that I've been on especially bad terms with money these past few years: I haven't seen any lying about in boxes recently!"

Just as one of them made this last remark they saw passing by them three carts loaded with chests of money, guarded by six men, each of whom bore a lantern marked with the household crest of a chevron and three stars. Behind them walked two men who appeared to be clerks, who were talking in some such terms as the following:

"They say money's short in this world, but there's plenty of it where you find it. This consignment of money on these carts is what our old master has set aside as pocket money for his aged mother. It was first deposited in the strongroom in the first year of Meireki[3] in the fourth month, and it's making its appearance today for the first time since then: it's out for an airing after the gloom of its long imprisonment. This money reminds me of a girl who was made a nun at birth: it has never been caressed by a man nor enjoyed a good time; furthermore, it's destined to go to the temple in the end."

Splitting their sides with laughter over their own joke, the men went on talking: "Today as I was taking this money out of storage, I happened to look across into the strongroom of the house annex just opposite. There were stacks and stacks of money chests with labels on them dating back to the Kan'ei era.[4] It's a marvel how such enormous wealth could ever have been accumulated in a single generation. Generally speaking, before all else rich men of this world have the reputation of being misers, and it usually takes plenty of scheming to become rich. Our master, on the contrary, is in every way as generous and liberal as a born lord. Although he has lived in the

[3] 1655.
[4] 1624–1644.

lap of luxury all his life, he is still just as rich as he ever was. He seems to be the very embodiment of good fortune.

"Up until now he was content to enjoy retirement in the home of his eldest son, but now that his second son has a house of his own he has changed his mind and prefers to live with him. Since in this family the old man's will is law, starting last eleventh month they began moving his things, and these money chests are the last load to be moved. Eleven maids were dispatched from the main house of the eldest son to wait on the old man. At the same time, seven cats moved along with him carried in a palanquin, just like so many human beings.

"On the twenty-first of this month, as is his custom, the master made presents of new clothes to his employees: forty-eight suits of clothes for the men, fifty-one for the women, and twenty-seven for small and middle-sized boys and girls—a grand total of one hundred and twenty-six. They were all ordered from the Sasaya, and without exception every single employee was given an outfit. Think of what they must have cost: enough money to set a man up in business!

"As for the young master, yesterday when the chief performer of female roles in a kabuki troupe came to pay his respects and in the course of conversation complained that they'd be unable to present this year's first theatrical performance for lack of funds, the master loaned him five hundred *ryō* of gold on the spot.

"Because they don't know that such wealth exists in this great capital, bill-collectors take the effort to carefully count up paltry payments of a hundred *mon*. As for our master and his brother, since we entered service in this household we have never at any time seen either one of them so much as touch money with his own hands. Of course, they have no idea how rich they actually are, for they leave all such business details to their head clerks, nine in number."

Conversing in this fashion, the two men now entered the grounds of an imposing-looking house, and after announcing that the retired master's money had arrived, they stored it in the strongroom.

The year man of this household, after seeing to it that a sacred candle had been lit for the gods of each altar there, asked if he should do the same for each strongroom. The master pointed at him and laughed, saying, "What a green year man we have here! For the owner of a mere thousand *kan* or so to burn candles at the corners of his strongroom might be quite appropriate. But if we started doing that here, we would have to light twenty-five or twenty-six candles. Does he need to light so many?"

The poor fellows who had followed along behind the procession of carts to the house were standing by envying its wealthy appearance. They continued to watch as the money chests were carried into the house one after another and stacked on the dirt floor near the entrance. The men accompanying the consignment of money, who seemed to be clerks of an exchange shop, begged the head clerk of the wealthy household to store the money away safely in one of the strong rooms. They tried their best to persuade him, pleading on their knees. But the head clerk resolutely refused to take it in, reminding them:

"Every year we have been telling you people, and by now you ought to be well aware of it, that on New Year's Eve we will not take money in from any source after four o'clock. It's a nuisance to have to bother with such a small sum of money, and that so late at night."

After a thousand apologies, however, and extensive flattery, the messengers finally succeeded in persuading the clerk to accept it. Turning over to him the three chests of money containing the sum total of six hundred and seventy *kan*, they took the receipt for it with virtually unbounded gratitude and at last went home.

The chests of money, since the strong rooms were already shut fast, were piled up behind the cauldron in the kitchen. That's where this large fortune saw the old year out: on the dirt floor of the kitchen, just as though it had been a bunch of stones or roof tiles.

The Kitchen Floor
Parties of Nara

THERE is something good and interesting about having the same peddler return year after year and getting to know him over a period of years. There is a fishmonger who until recently visited Nara over a span of some twenty-four or twenty-five years. And as he sold only octopuses he became known as "Octopus" Hachisuke. He had a goodly number of customers, which enabled him to support his family of three; yet never on a New Year's Eve had he been able to see the old year out with even so small a balance on hand as five hundred *mon*. All that he could manage on New Year's Day was to feed his family and have a bowl of *zōni*.

Since his youth "Octopus" Hachisuke had been alert to the art of getting on in life. When his widowed mother asked him to buy her a brazier he dared to take some commission from her for the service. As for the neighbors, needless to say, he would never do anything for them for nothing. Even at a time when the midwife was urgently needed, he was reluctant to fetch her until he had been treated to a hasty meal. This world is indeed filled with greed, yet that of Hachisuke was so outstanding that even when he went to buy cloth for a shroud for a deceased member of the *nenbutsu*[1]-chanting confraternity of which he himself was a member, he insisted on getting his commission on the purchase. Why, he was the sort of man who was actually glad when someone died, for then he could gouge out their eyes for his profit. Still, for all his selfishness, he remained poor; which appeared to be no more than divine justice.

Here in Japan an octopus normally has eight legs, but from the very first day Hachisuke began peddling in Nara he made it a practice to slice off one leg and sell seven-legged octopuses. His cunning practice went unnoticed by practically everybody. Then he contracted to sell those single legs to the keeper of a food stand in Matsubara, whose wont it was to buy nothing but sliced-off legs. How full of avaricious thoughts is the human mind!

Now there is a proverb which declares that "You may cheat seventy-five times, but no more," for the time is bound to come when your dishonesty will be discovered. Last New Year's Eve Hachisuke cut off *two* legs from each octopus and sold six-legged ones. But still his regular customers were so busy that they did not notice the amputations. He went right on selling maimed octopuses in this fashion until he came to the middle of the Tegai district. There he was summoned to a house surrounded by a fence made of crisscrossed bamboo laths, where they bought two octopuses. As he was leaving, the master of the house, whose head was clean-shaven like that of a Buddhist priest, glanced up from his game of *go*.

---

[1] A formula invoking Amida Buddha (Sanskrit Amitābha) repeated by practitioners of Pure Land Buddhism.

Leaving off his game, he came over to Hachisuke to look more closely at the octopuses, remarking that somehow they seemed to taper off at the end. All of a sudden he thundered out, "In which one of the seven seas did you catch these anomalies? Never since the age of the gods has any book made mention of six-legged octopuses. It's a shame how you've been cheating all the people of Nara. I'll remember your face well, fishmonger!"

"Very well!" retorted Hachisuke. "And I in turn refuse to sell my octopuses to such a lazy fellow as you who plays *go* on New Year's Eve."

Later this incident was made public knowledge, though no one seems to know exactly how it got into circulation.

Since Nara was not a very large town, in every nook and corner where people gossiped the infamy of "Leg-Cutting" Hachisuke was spread, until he was no longer able to peddle there—and all because of his inordinate greed.

In Nara it is much quieter on New Year's Eve than it is in either Kyoto or Osaka. People pay for their credit purchases with all the cash they have on hand; so if they say they can't pay a bill, the collectors accept their word for it and go their way, not tarrying to press for payment. By ten o'clock in the evening, having ended their payment business, all the people of Nara set about enjoying the New Year atmosphere by holding what is called a "Kitchen Floor Party." They make a fire under the cauldron in the kitchen and spread straw matting on the earthen floor. Then, gathering from their respective rooms, the entire household, from the master on down to the lowliest maidservant, seat themselves casually on the matting in the kitchen. According to local custom, they take out rice cakes molded into a round shape in rings of cut bamboo, and after broiling them eat them all together. It is a fine sight to see, and one which gives the impression that the household is quite well-off.

Outcaste men who live outside the town start celebrating the season by visiting first of all the home of Inaba, a retainer of the noble priest of the Daijōin Temple. After that they go around town chanting, "Wealth, wealth, wealth!" and every household hands out rice cakes and copper coins. Much the same is true in the case of those called "evil-chasers" in places like Osaka.

When New Year's Day dawns, men sell printed pictures of Daikoku, the god of wealth, calling out, "Get your lucky fortune! Get your bales of luck!" At dawn of the second day they sell prints of Ebisu, another god of fortune, calling out meantime, "Get your Ebisu here!"

And finally on the dawn of the third day it is Bishamon's pictures that they sell, crying, "Bishamon! Get your Bishamon here!" In short, for three days they sell the gods of prosperity.

As for the rites observed on New Year's Day, the people of Nara, before making their calls upon one another, visit Kasuga Shrine. On this occasion they invite all their kinfolk, even to the remotest cousins, and make the occasion quite a merry one. The larger the company they gather, the greater their reputation in the eyes of the world.

No matter where you go, you will discover that it is a most enviable state to be rich. The dealers in the sun-bleached cotton cloth of Nara sell their goods to the drapers of Kyoto on credit, collecting the money on New Year's Eve. That very same night, as soon as they have balanced their account books, they leave Kyoto for Nara with the many thousands of *kan* of silver which they have taken in for their bleached cotton, making their way by the light of a train of burning torches. The day is just dawning as the procession reaches Nara, where they store the gold and silver in strong rooms, usually finishing the balancing of their mutual debts and credits on the fifth of the first month.[2]

In a secluded village of Yamato there once lived a group of poor ronin who, finding it hard to tide over the year end, thought it a good idea to plunder the procession of money chests on their way to Nara. So the gang of four plotted in secret to assault the party at the risk of their lives. The attack was successful, but when they broke open one of the chests they were dismayed to discover that it contained no petty cash such as they might use for "drink money," but only large sums, such as thirty- and fifty-*kan* pieces. They examined all the chests, one after another, but not daring to appropriate such large sums for drink money, in the end they abandoned them.

Then the ronin robbers shifted their place of operations to the Dark Pass between Osaka and Nara, to lie in wait for travelers returning from Osaka. Along came a man of small stature carrying on his shoulder a package wrapped in straw matting. "How very intelligent of him," they agreed, "to carry a heavy thing as though it were light. Surely he must have money hidden in it." So they attacked him, but as they made off with his package the man cried out that it would be of no immediate use to them.

When the four robbers opened the package, imagine their surprise and consternation to discover inside nothing but dried herring roe!

---

[2]The day of the first market of the year for selling sun-bleached Nara cloth (SNKBZ p. 434 note 3).

Swapping Houses

THE VERY water sounded busy on the twenty-ninth night of the twelfth month as waves on the river at Fushimi approached the bank like the coming New Year while their backwash left it like the year about to end. The ferry for Osaka was about to leave, and since the passengers were in a greater hurry than usual they loudly urged the boatman to cast off at once. Himself well aware that the New Year was at hand, the boatman replied, "Don't worry. I know as well as you that only two days are left in this year—today and tomorrow." With that he at last unmoored the boat and set off from the dock at Kyōbashi.

Ordinarily the passengers on the Osaka-bound ferry would not be silent. Some would be repeating brothel-quarter rumors, or telling rapid-fire stories, or be singing shamisen ballads or *jōruri*, or chanting passages from nō plays or *kōwakamai*, while others would be amusing themselves with imitations of popular actors. But tonight they seemed both silent and morose.

The silence was broken occasionally by someone chanting the *nenbutsu*. Or someone would vent his spleen by complaining that in our short span of life in this floating world to await the New Year was just like waiting for one's time to come. Other passengers, unable to get their usual sleep, looked serious and worried. Then a fellow who appeared to be a petty clerk started singing loudly and long-windedly some ballads whose words he had picked up in a teahouse employing prostitutes. So off-key did he hum the shamisen accompaniment, and so grotesquely did he mark time by wagging his head that the company was thoroughly disgusted with his performance.

Meanwhile the ferryboat had progressed as far as the Little Yodo Bridge. As the boatman, guided by a lamp marking the channel under the bridge, slipped the vessel between the piers stern foremost, a man who, awakening from a nap assumed a sober attitude, spoke out in a manner that seemed to indicate that he considered himself the only intelligent person aboard:

"Look here," he exclaimed, "if a man works day and night all the year round with unremitting diligence just like that water wheel over there, at the year end he will be able to balance his accounts to conform to his advance calculations. But if he is idle the rest of the year, it does no good for him to start struggling just before the end of the year."

All the other passengers, who had been listening to him, nodded their heads in approval. Among them was a man who lived on Inn Street in Hyōgo. "Those words of yours went straight to my heart," he said. "Since I live near the sea I can catch plenty of fish and live comfortably. Every year, however, at the year end I discover that somehow my income has fallen just a little short of my expenditures. For the past fourteen or fifteen years now I have been accustomed to visit my maternal aunt in Ōtsu to ask her for some petty cash—say, seventy or eighty *monme*—anyway I've never asked her for a hundred. But this year for some reason she was so fed up with my annual requests that she turned me down flat. Since I had been taking it for granted that I could get the loan from her as easily as picking up something I'd left behind, her refusal hit me pretty hard. At present I have no idea how I'll manage to tide over the year end at home."

Another passenger spoke up: "I brought my little brother up to Kyoto to see an actor in the kabuki district of the dry riverbed at Shijō with whom I had some acquaintance. I had hoped to apprentice him to the actor's theatrical troupe and use the money that would be advanced to get safely past the year end. The boy's looks are beyond compare, if I do say so myself, so I felt sure that some day he would become the troupe's leading performer of women's roles. Sad to say, however, the actor declined to take him on, saying his ears were just a little too small for a regular actor.[1] So all there was left for me to do was to bring my brother back from Kyoto.

"One thing I learned, however, and that is that there are a lot of people in this world. Every day people bring in as many as twenty or thirty boys between eleven and thirteen years old who are of handsome figure and good manners and well suited to the stage. In strict confidence the agents are saying that some of them are sons of ronin and physicians. That is, their fathers are from good families, but since they have found it hard to tide over this year end they want to place their sons in a company of actors. The manager can choose any he wants for a term of ten years for a consideration ranging from one *kan* to thirty *monme* of silver. In point of fairness of complex-

[1] As opposed to one specializing in prostitution (*SNKBZ* p. 438 note 14).

ion and cleverness, boys from other districts can't hold a candle to those from the Kyoto-Osaka area. So I have to return
home out of money for travel expenses."

Then another fellow spoke up and said, "My parents be-
queathed me a mandala from the ink brush of Saint Nichiren
himself. Once a man in Uji wanted it so badly that he told me
he would pay me any price I asked for it, but at the time I was
reluctant to part with it. This year, however, being pinched for
money, I went all the way to Uji to sell it to the man. In the
meantime, somehow he had been converted to the Jōdo sect
and I found that he wasn't at all interested in the mandala. As
my expectations were dashed to the ground, I felt quite embarrassed. Now I have no alternative plan of procedure. In any
case, it will be so annoying to return home and meet the im-
portunate bill collectors that I intend to go straight to Mt.
Kōya without stopping in Osaka at all. The omniscient Kōbō
Daishi[2] must think it all very funny!"

A fourth man now spoke up and said, "I used to sell rice to
the weavers of Kyoto on credit and see the old year out without a care in the world. The arrangement I had with them was
that, charging a service fee, I would supply them in the
twelfth month with rice on credit which cost forty-five *monme*
per *koku*. At the end of the third month they paid me fif-
ty-eight *monme* per *koku* for it. I ran this business every year
until this one, when the cloth-workers had a meeting and decided not to buy their rice from me, saying that my interest
rate of thirteen *monme* per *koku* for three months was exorbitant. They would rather celebrate the New Year without my
rice, they said. So after going to the trouble and expense of

---

[2] The founder of the Shingon temple complex on Mt. Kōya, also known as
Kūkai (774–835).

shipping the rice upriver all the way to Toba, I had to store it there and return home."

Undoubtedly, none of the somber passengers on this ferry would be able to spend New Year's Eve at home. Now, it is impossible for such men to call on friends and stay with them overnight, for unlike ordinary days, on that special day people are extremely busy. The daylight hours can be spent viewing prayer tablets at temples and shrines, but when night falls they have nowhere to go. So it is said that those who are heavily in debt usually keep an understanding mistress in whose quarters they may hide on the five days in the year when the settlement of accounts is imminent. Although such may be possible for those who have plenty of money at their disposal, it is far beyond the reach of the poor.

There was a man who from early evening began singing shamisen ballads in a leisurely manner, much to the envy of another man, who said to him, "You must already have settled all your outstanding debts." At this the singer burst out laughing and replied, "You all seem to be unaware of a tactic that can enable one to keep a roof over his head, while at the same time doing someone else a favor on this particular day. Two or three years ago someone hit upon the idea of temporarily swapping houses with a friend to tide both parties over the year end. When bill collectors call, each of the friends pretends that he is another cold-hearted bill collector and thus addresses the mistress of the house: "Madam, my bill is of a different variety from the ordinary debt. I'll settle this account with him even if I have to rip it out of his guts!" When any listening bill collector hears such ferocious language used, he gives up clamoring for the immediate payment of his bill and quits the place forthwith.

Such, in brief, is an outline of a recently devised scheme for thwarting bill collectors, which goes by the name of "men swapping houses." Since it is not yet widely known, it still works.

The Pillar Rice-Cakes
of Nagasaki

THE LAST day of the eleventh month is the deadline for Chinese ships to leave Nagasaki; after that day it becomes a deserted seaport. But during the period when the China trade is allowed, the people of Nagasaki generally earn enough to live on the rest of the year. According to their degrees of fortune, rich and poor alike live comfortably and do not have to keep track of every minute expenditure. As a general thing, since they buy for cash, when bills fall due before festival days, there is not much fuss. Even with the New Year approaching they go right on drinking their saké as usual. Indeed, in this port city life seems easier. Even in the twelfth month people do not rush about, nor are any twelfth-month beggars, such as we ordinarily see in the Kyoto-Osaka area, to be found in the streets. Only by the Ise calendar are the people of Nagasaki aware of the coming of the New Year, and in conformity with time-honored custom, they make it a practice to clean their houses from top to bottom on the thirteenth of the twelfth month. The bamboo used for sweeping up around the house is tied to the ridge of the roof and left there until the next house-cleaning day.

Each home, according to its own individual custom, makes rice-cakes, the most interesting of which are called "pillar rice-cakes." This kind of rice-cake is made last of all and then stuck on the central pillar of the house (whence its name), to be roasted at the festival of Sagichō, which comes on the fifteenth of the first month and marks the end of the New Year celebrations.

Individual local customs, I have said, are quite interesting. In Nagasaki again, they set up in the kitchen what they call "lucky poles" in a horizontal position. On them are hung all kinds of foods: yellowtails, dried sea cucumbers, skewered abalone, wild geese, wild ducks, pheasants, salted porgies, salted sardines, edible seaweed, codfish, bonitos, bundles of burdock, and other foods, all of which will be served at table during the first three days of the New Year.

After dark on New Year's Eve, beggar women, their faces painted red, visit from house to house, bearing trays on which are placed clay figures of the gods of fortune Ebisu or Daikoku or a heap of coarse salt. They call out, "The tide has come in from the sea lying in the direction from which good luck will come this year!" This is because the harbor is the most important place in that city.

Although it is the custom everywhere that a New Year's gift not be too expensive, the ones given out in Nagasaki are mere trifles: to men a fan, fifty of which cost one *monme*; and to women a pinch of tea leaves enfolded in a piece of paper. Since this apparent stinginess is the custom of the entire city, no one should be thought the less of for observing it.

Whatever you may say, there's no place like home. It is quite natural, then, for merchants of every province visiting

Nagasaki near the end of the year to try to wrap up their business as soon as possible, in anticipation of celebrating the New Year in their hometowns.

In Kyoto there lived a small-scale merchant who dealt in thread and yarn. For twenty years he had made it a regular practice to visit Nagasaki annually on business. Being shrewder than anyone else, whenever he started on his journey he invariably ate a last meal at home, just before he left Kyoto, for neither on land nor on sea was he willing to spend a single *zeni* more than was necessary on anything at all. During his stay in Nagasaki he never even took a peep at the brothel quarter of Maruyama. So even in his dreams he never saw how elegant Kinzan looked when she was seated, or how white was the back of Kachō's neck. At night when he retired he set an abacus close beside his pillow, and slept with an account book in his hand. He was forever trying to figure out how he could make a killing by cheating some gullible Chinese trader. But nowadays Chinese merchants understand and speak Japanese, and although they may have a lot of surplus cash on hand they won't lend it unless they have house mortgages as security. They also know that it is more profitable to buy a house that will bring a good return when rented out than it is to lend money for interest. They are now so smart that they can no longer be considered easy marks. Smarter still, however, are the native merchants of Nagasaki, who will not allow anyone to enjoy a "soft" job.

If cleverness were the only requisite for getting rich, this man from Kyoto would have been a millionaire, but he was not blessed with that *sine qua non* of riches—good luck. There were many other Kyoto thread dealers who had begun visiting Nagasaki on business about the same time as he had and who had amassed great fortunes. Thereafter they would send their clerks down to Nagasaki in their places, they themselves remaining at ease in Kyoto, beguiling the time now with sight-seeing, now with flower-viewing, and now with the fervent frequenting of prostitutes. One of them ascribed the secret of his success to what he called the "merchant spirit," which meant the constant observation of the world of affairs and trying to determine in advance what articles would rise in price the following year. Then he resolutely set about cornering that particular market, and thus by speculation made a large fortune. If one did not stake his all on the game, he would never get rich.

Now our thread dealer calculated very closely the difference between the purchase price in Nagasaki and the selling price in Kyoto. And his figures were never even a little bit off. However, as he was engaged in a sound business venture, he never made a killing. The margin of profit that he did realize was eaten up by the repayment of interest on loans as well as the principal. In short, though his labors were great and painstaking, it was another who reaped the profits.

Every New Year's Eve he was in the habit of putting up at an inn in Hashimoto, where he would see the old year out. It was just an old family custom, he would explain, but the truth of the matter was that he couldn't stay home because he couldn't pay his debts. If possible, he would have preferred celebrating the New Year at home in Kyoto. Ruminating on the vicissitudes of life, he came to the conclusion that on the one hand his small-scale business would probably never cause him any really serious loss; yet on the other hand, as other people rightly remarked, it would never bring him in any very large profit. "This year," he said to himself, "I must devise some plan beyond my regular business and make a large profit." Having so determined in his mind, he went down to Nagasaki, all the while cudgeling his brain to hit upon some good scheme. But after all, since only money begets money, there seemed to be no way to create it *ex nihilo*.

Wasn't there some attraction or freak of nature that he could exhibit next spring? He found it hard to think of anything, for already a variety of novelties had been created by the artisans of Kyoto and Osaka. Still, there might be just one article among the imports that would do. Anyhow, it had to be a very special kind of novelty, for anything less would be unprofitable. He considered the matter very carefully. Certain to be profitable, since none had ever been seen on any stage, was a baby giant lizard or a fire-eating ostrich. But such an anomaly was not to be obtained even in Nagasaki.

So secretly he sought out a Chinese trader and inquired if he happened to know of any rare thing in a foreign country. "Although I have heard of them," replied the Chinese trader, "never yet have I seen a phoenix, or the lightning god. After all, whatever is rare in Japan—such as aloeswood or ginseng—is equally rare in China. I have traversed thousands of miles of rough sea at the risk of my life and come all the way to Japan solely in search of one rare thing—money. Remember that in all the world there is nothing people want so much as money."

Considering this to be very sensible advice indeed, the merchant from Kyoto applied himself all the more diligently to his business. But at the same time he bought various kinds of exotic birds in Nagasaki. Yet when he returned to Kyoto with the birds, since there were already similar ones that had been put on display, they failed to bring him in any profit. The peacocks which he brought back, however, though already familiar to the public, were still popular, which enabled him to barely break even on the capital he had invested in the sideline business. Which all goes to show that you should stick to what you know.

A Night Auction
at the Year-End

NOT A year passes without people complaining that the times are bad and business is poor. But suppose you try to sell something that has a market price of ten *monme* at your own price of nine *monme* and eight *bu*. Immediately you will receive orders amounting to a thousand *kan*. On the other hand, if you offer to buy for ten *monme* something which ordinarily sells for nine *monme* and eight *bu*, you will immediately be offered two thousand *kan's* worth. How wonderfully magnanimous are the merchants in large cities! The fact is that buying and selling depends entirely on the way people calculate.

People who maintain that what this world lacks is money must never have seen the living quarters of the rich. On the contrary, money exists abundantly in this world. This is proved by the patent fact that for the past thirty years people all over the country have been growing more and more prosperous. A house formerly thatched with straw is now shingled. The houses at the Fuwa checkpoint, described in an old poem as having the moonlight filtering in,[1] are now roofed with tile and whitewashed. Besides, they have a strongroom and a storehouse. The sliding screens of their halls are no longer covered with gold and silver dust, for this is considered too gaudy; they are painted with gold and silver paint. Moreover, the pictures on them are drawn in India ink, elegantly enough. And so far as taste goes, they are quite the same as those of residents of the capital.

Again we learn from an old poem that formerly the salt-burning women of Nada "didn't even wear a little box-wood comb" in their hair.[2] But nowadays even such seashore dwellers are very particular about their kimono and eager to hear about and see for themselves the latest fashions of Kyoto and Osaka. They know that a kimono design of small pine trees is no longer stylish, and that the new mode is a design of dwarf bamboo in the evening sun. Also it is a fact that while suburban dwellers in even Kyoto and Osaka wear kimono featuring an outdated design of small paulownia flowers and squirrel's foot ferns, the very latest dyed fabrics from Kyoto may be seen in the countryside. Nowadays it is amusing, however, to see the word "cuckoo" dyed on the shoulder part of a kimono of obsolete design, or to see the dark red-dyed grape-vines clinging to their trellises, though when these patterns first hit the market they seemed stylish and fresh.

At any rate, wherever you may be, if only you have plenty of money, you may do as you please. On the other hand, a poor man has little chance of tiding over the year end no matter how hard he tries to think up a means of doing so. If there's no money—well, there's just no money—that's all! No

---

[1] *Shin kokin waka shū* no. 1601.
[2] *Tales of Ise* no. 87.

matter how hard a man may search the shelf, he can't find even a single *mon* unless he previously put it there himself. Hence it is highly advisable to practice economy all the year round. If a man cuts back on his tobacco consumption enough to save just one *mon* a day, in one year he will have saved three hundred sixty *mon*, and in ten years three *kan* and six hundred *mon*. If he economizes in everything—tea, firewood, miso, salt and the like—by such frugality he will be able to save thirty-six *monme* in a year, no matter how impoverished his daily life may be. In ten years the savings will amount to three hundred sixty *monme*, and when you add interest, in thirty years the total will mount up to more than eight *kan*. In short, one should take care every day of one's life and never be negligent in even a trifle. Especially must one remember the old proverb, "At every meal with drink poverty flourishes."

There was once a poor maker of nails who barely managed to live from hand to mouth. Never a day passed but he bought eight *mon's* worth of saké three times a day, having it poured into a small bottle that had once been used to offer saké to the god Inari at the time of the Fire Festival. He continued to drink in this manner for forty-five years. The total quantity he consumed during these years amounted to forty *koku* and five *to*, supposing that the volume of saké he drank daily was two and a half *gō*. If the cost was twenty-four *mon* a day, counting twelve *monme* of silver as one *kan* of copper, over the years the sum total he spent for saké amounted to four *kan* and eight hundred and sixty *monme* of silver. When people made fun of this man, saying that if he were more temperate he would not be so poor, he would look at them coolly, just as though he were managing his household with success, and declare that no teetotaler had ever been known to build a storehouse. He then went right on drinking.

One New Year's Eve, this man had practically completed his preparation for the season, with the *Hōrai* decorations set out, when he discovered that there was no money left to buy his usual ration of saké. Since for forty-five years not a day had passed but that he was in his cups, to him the thought of facing the first day of the New Year without his saké was unbearable. If this should occur, New Year's Day would for him be devoid of meaning. So husband and wife put their heads together, but could think of no one who might lend them the drink money; nor had they anything that they might pawn. Finally they thought of a sedge hat, used the previous summer to keep off the heat of the sun, which still remained green and in good condition.

Summertime would not be coming around again for quite a while. A person could sell whatever he had for his convenience, couldn't he? There seemed to be no other way to meet the immediate crisis.

So the man took the sedge hat to the night auction of secondhand goods, which was by this time in full swing. All the sellers, judging by their appearance, were suffering from burdens of debt and had no one to turn to for relief. The auctioneer, spurred on by his ten percent commission, was bidding up the prices with vigor. The things he offered for sale at this year-end auction, though mute, spoke eloquently of how badly their owners were in need of money.

One article being auctioned seemed to be the New Year's kimono of a girl of twelve or thirteen, with a seashore design tie-dyed onto a spring green background. The lining was pink. The cotton kimono was well padded, but the cuffs had not yet been stitched up. When the bidding stopped it had sold for six *monme* and three and a half *bu*, a paltry price when one considers that the lining alone could not be made for so little money.

Next in order, half of a small yellowtail caught in the sea off Tango province[3] was brought out. It went for two *monme* and a half *bu*. After that a mosquito net made to cover the space of two tatami mats was put up for auction. It was bid up from eight *monme* to thirty-three and a half *monme*, but the owner refused to sell it at that price. Thereupon someone laughed and said, "You're not likely to make a profit off *that*. Anyhow, you must be quite well-off to have been able to hold onto your mosquito net all the way to New Year's Eve!"

The next item for sale was a text written on ten sheets of wax-treated paper pasted together to form a long scroll, and to which was affixed the signature and seal of an authorized practitioner of the Son'en school of calligraphy. It was bid up from one *bu* to five. The auctioneer, complaining that the bid was too low, cried out, "Why, the paper alone must be worth at least three *monme*."

"Yes, it might be," came a voice from the crowd. "If there weren't any writing on it, but the useless calligraphy text has reduced its value to less than five *bu*. Whoever the writer was, I say he's just a 'breechcloth artist.'"

"What do you mean by a 'breechcloth artist'?" asked the auctioneer.

"Well, just as no man lacks a breechcloth," he answered with a sneer, "these days anyone born a man can write at least as well as this fellow!"

"Careful, these are fragile!" cried the auctioneer when the next items were brought out: ten sashimi plates of cheap Chinese porcelain with old letters written by well-known prosti-

---

[3] Yellowtail caught in the waters off Ine-chō in Yosa-gun (then in Tango province, now in Kyoto prefecture) were especially prized (*SNKBZ* p. 455 note 13).

tutes of Kyoto and Osaka put between them as packing. Busy as the people were, they still could not resist the temptation to read them. The letters which had been written in the twelfth month, they discovered, contained no mention whatever of love or tenderness, but were begging only for money—with appropriate and polite apologies, of course.

"Both love and death cost money," remarked the auctioneer. "The owner of these plates," he continued, "must once have been known in the brothel quarter as a big spender. Why, each one of these letters must have cost him at least one piece of silver, in which case they must be worth more than the plates are."

At this everyone present roared with laughter.

Following that, an image of Fudō, the deity who sits amidst blazing fire, was brought forth for sale, together with a vajra, a brass tray for scattered flower offerings, a hand bell for Buddhist rituals, a holy staff,[4] and an old altar used for the fire-burning ritual.[5] These were greeted with the derisive comment that it looked as if Fudō was unable to pray that he himself enjoy wealth and high position.

At this point the sedge hat was put up for auction. Someone in the audience seeing it cried out, disregarding the fact that its owner was present, "Oh, what a shame! The owner must have expected to wear it many more summers, because it's kept in a sack made of tissue paper. What a thrifty fellow he must be!"

The first bid for the hat was three *mon*, but by the time it was sold the bid had risen to fourteen *mon*. As the money was handed to the seller, he swore in the name of some god or

---

[4] A *khakkhara*.
[5] *Goma*.

Buddha that he had bought it for thirty-six *mon* in the fifth month and had worn it only once: on the festival day of the blue-faced Vajrayakṣa. The self-disclosure of his disgrace was truly funny to hear.

At the final auction of the night, a man bought twenty-five cases of year-end gift fans and a box of tobacco for two *monme* and seven *bu*. On returning home he opened the box. Inside, hidden under the tobacco, he found three gold *ryō* pieces—an entirely unexpected stroke of good fortune it was for him, indeed.

Blinds from
Inkbrush Handles

A CERTAIN man who had learned an unforgettable lesson from the trying experiences of the year end made up his mind that once the three days of the New Year's holiday had passed, from the fourth day of the first month onward he would never be negligent in his work. He resolved to deal strictly on a cash-and-carry basis, and would do without fish at table unless he was sure he could afford it. Moreover, during the year he would balance all his accounts faithfully on every one of the five annual settlement days. He lived thus a whole year, ever keeping in mind how exacting bill collectors are.

It was not long before another New Year rolled around. This year, he thought, he would change the dates of household events and as early as the second day of the first month he would perform the binding of a new account book for the year, an event which his family had previously celebrated on the tenth day; also he would take inventory on the third day rather than the fifth as had been their custom hitherto. It was not a good idea, he thought, even to go out of the house, because if he did he might have to spend money unexpectedly, or someone might ask him to go see the sights or to visit a temple or shrine, which would mean a whole precious day wasted. He spoke to others only on business, and all day and every day he occupied his time with business calculations.

"Since we live in a world where little profit is to be made," he thought, "the most important thing is to economize on household expenditures." So in the third month, when servants' contracts come up for renewal, he discharged the kitchen maid and thereafter had his wife put on an apron and take her place. As for himself, in the daytime he occupied his usual place as master in the shop, but after dark when the shop was closed he worked along with his apprentice boy at the treadle of the rice-polishing mortar. Furthermore, he would usually wash his feet with freshly drawn water without bothering to heat it up. Nevertheless, this man was dogged by poverty, for in spite of all his economizing his business dropped off, and he melted away like ice in the sun.

It has been well said that a one-*shō* ladle can't hold more than one *shō*. Such was the case with a certain priestess of Kumano, who used to show people pictures of Paradise and Hell and sing popular songs till her breath gave out. Despite her desperate solicitation for alms, however, she was barely able to fill her one-*shō* ladle with rice doled out in charity. The longing which people have for a happy future life exhibits itself in varying degrees.

Last winter the priest Kōkei, abbot of the Ryūshōin subtemple of Tōdaiji in Nara, began a journey to raise contributions to rebuild that temple's Great Buddha Hall. He would not solicit at all from unbelievers. He just walked silently along the way, accepting purely voluntary donations. Never-

theless, though like the priestess of Kumano he carried a one-
shō ladle, people donated one *kan* of mon coins each step of
the way, and ten *kan* every ten steps. Some even gave gold and
silver. The blessings of the Buddha shine just as brightly as
the coins one contributes to him, and the present age is the
bright and shining noon of Buddhism. Besides, since the re-
building of the Great Buddha Hall was a special event, members of every Buddhist sect showed great eagerness to
contribute to it. Ranging from one-*mon* donations by the poor
who live on the outskirts of town to gifts of ten thousand *kan*
of *mon* coins by the very rich, totaled together they have already equaled the cost of a round pillar worth twelve *kan* of
silver used in the reconstruction. Which goes to show you,
one ought to be careful in everything and look for ways to
save money, no matter how small the amount.

By the way, those who accumulate a fortune are by nature
different from others. There was a man who sent his son to a
school from his ninth through his twelfth year to learn calligraphy. During these years the boy saved the handles of all his
writing brushes, as well as those used by others. Then in the
spring that he became thirteen years old he made blinds of
them and sold as many as three of them, at one and a half
monme apiece, thus earning four and a half *monme* of silver.
"This son of mine," thought the fond father, "is no ordinary
person," and he said as much to the monk who had been
teaching his son calligraphy. The monk, apparently not sharing the father's enthusiasm, said to him:

"During my life I have taught hundreds of children, and
not one of the all too clever ones like your son grew up to be
rich. None turned out to be a beggar, either, but they are now
living at an economic level below the median. Smartness is
not the only factor for success, you know. Besides, it is a mis-

take to think that your son is the only smart boy in the world. There are boys smarter than he is when it comes to dealing with money. For example, I know a boy who swept the classroom every day after practice was over, whether he was on duty that day or not. As he did so, he picked up all the sheets of paper thrown away by the other boys, smoothed them out, and sold them to a maker of folding screens. This was a better idea than making blinds of brush handles, for it brought in cash right away. But even that was not so good, either. Another boy I know brought extra sheets of paper along with him to his lessons, and when other boys ran out of paper, he loaned them some, charging interest of one hundred per cent a day. He must have made an enormous yearly profit off this! All these boys had absorbed such worldly-wise methods from the experiences of their profit-seeking parents. Their ideas were not the spontaneous product of their own minds.

"On the other hand, there was a boy whose parents always admonished him to devote himself exclusively to calligraphy, for they said that in the future it would stand him in good stead. Quite obedient to his parents, he devoted himself day and night to reading and writing, until in time he surpassed his seniors in brush writing. No doubt he will grow up to be a wealthy merchant, for he has learned how to concentrate on whatever task he has to do.

"After all, it is rare for one to succeed if he abandons the hereditary family business to start a new one. The case is the same with boys learning calligraphy: they must practice brush writing to the exclusion of everything else. It is uselessly greedy to set aside one's writing practice at a tender age and devote oneself to moneymaking, and it is shameful for a child whose assigned role is to study calligraphy to not be good at it. It cannot be truthfully said that your son's attitude is good.

After all, when one is young it is best to pick flowers and fly kites, and later to settle down when one is old enough to learn the business. Now just remember what this old man of seventy has been telling you, and keep your eye on these boys to see what becomes of them in the future."

The predictions of the master of calligraphy did indeed come true. When these smart boys grew up and had to make their own living, they tried out various new ideas and kept on failing. The one who had made blinds out of old inkbrush handles devised a way of attaching wooden protectors to the soles of straw sandals to be used in winter when the streets were muddy, but his idea enjoyed only a brief vogue. The boy who had gathered waste paper devised a method of coating unglazed pottery with resin to keep it from absorbing oil, but on New Year's Eve his income barely enabled him to light one lamp. On the other hand, the boy who had devoted himself wholeheartedly to calligraphy, though seemingly slow-witted, was broad-minded by nature. He invented a method for keeping barrels of oil from congealing while they were being shipped to Edo by boat in mid-winter, by inserting a bit of pepper in each barrel. From this invention he realized enormous profits and greeted the next New Year as a rich man. The two had both been thinking of the same thing—oil. But one of them had thought in terms of earthenware vessels, while the other thought in terms of barrels of oil.

How wide the gulf separating human minds!

Lord Heitarō

"WE TRUST in the Buddha in order to make a living," is an old proverb which still holds good.

Every year on the evening ushering in the first day of spring, the story of Saint Shinran's disciple Lord Heitarō is told in all the temples of the Jōdo Shinshū sect of Buddhism. Year after year the story does not vary, yet each time people hear it they are impressed anew. So usually many people, old and young, men and women, gather to listen to it.

One year the eve of the first day of spring happened to fall on New Year's Eve.[1] As a result, the voices of the bill collectors were mingled with the incantations of the men casting out devils, while the clink of money balances blended with the sound of soybeans thrown to drive out demons before the start of the new season. The eerie effect of this reminded one of the expression, "A demon in the dark"; it was truly terrify-

---

[1] This occurred in 1662 (*SNKBZ* p. 463 note 13.)

ing. At a Jōdo Shinshū temple in Osaka the drumbeat marking the start of the service sounded and the priest placed
lanterns before the Buddha image, then awaited the arrival of
worshipers. Yet even after the bell marking the arrival of
nighttime had tolled, only three visitors were to be seen in the
hall. The priest at last completed the rituals the occasion required, then, after pondering for a moment the state of the
world, addressed the worshipers in these words:

"Because tonight happens to be the deadline for the settlement of all debts of the old year, people seem to be too busy
to attend the services. I should think, however, that even tonight any grandmother who has retired from active household
management would have nothing to do. When Amida Buddha arrives from the other world to ferry her across to it, she
cannot refuse to get in the boat. How foolish people are!
What a pity, what a shame to neglect the services of the Buddha! But now it seems of little use to preach a sermon to only
three people. Although these are sacred services to the Buddha, a few material considerations must also be taken into account. Since the offerings of you three will scarcely pay for the
lamp oil burned, it seems uneconomical to preach. Would you
kindly take back your offerings and go home? To have come
here at a time when people are so absorbed in their worldly
affairs is none the less praiseworthy on your part and a sign of
true devotion. You may rest assured that the Buddha will see
to it that your attendance tonight will not have been in vain.
He will have it recorded in his golden ledger to balance your
accounts in the future life. So I beg you not to think that your
piety tonight has done you no good at all, for the Buddha is
all charity. This I speak in earnest. You may depend upon it
absolutely."

An old woman who had been listening began to shed tears

and said, "Your inspiring words have made me thoroughly ashamed of myself, I must confess that I did not come here from any pious motive. My only son has been neglecting his business, and until now each time that bills fall due he has managed to get by with some excuse or other, but this New Year's Eve there's no way he can talk his way out of paying. At last he asked me to come here, so that after I was gone he could make a racket, crying out that his old mother was missing. Then while the neighbors beat drums and rang bells all night long, he could go around pretending to be searching for me. Such was his scheme for tiding over the year end. He boasted that although claiming to look for a lost child was an old ploy for staving off bill collectors, shouting 'Come back Grandma!' instead was his own original touch. It is unfortunate for me that I have a son who is so good-for-nothing, but what a pity it is that I should sin unwillingly by giving my neighbors so much trouble!"

Another person, a man from the province of Ise, spoke up: "Fate is forever a mystery," he said. "At first I was quite a stranger in this big city for I had no relatives here. But since I was employed by a clerk of the Grand Shrine of Ise responsible for the subscribers living in Osaka, I would visit this city carrying on my back things to be delivered to them. Seeing what a prosperous city Osaka was, I thought that a family of two or three might easily make a living here doing something or other.

Fortunately I made the acquaintance of the widow of a seller of small articles who used to peddle his wares in Yamato Province. She was a sturdy, fair-skinned woman, with a two-year-old son. Thinking that with both of us working we might live comfortably, and that when I grew old I could depend upon the boy to provide for me, I married into her household, taking her surname.

"But less than half a year after we wed I lost what little money we had due to my lack of experience in peddling, and from the first of the twelfth month I have had to think seriously of finding another job. Meantime my wife would soothe her baby by cooing, 'Listen to me carefully, for you have ears. You must know that although your dead papa was a small man he was clever. He even cooked, which is a woman's task. He would let me go to bed early, while he sat up until dawn making straw sandals. He wouldn't buy himself a kimono, but he had new ones made for you and me to wear in the New Year season. This yellowish-brown one here brings back fond memories of him. Once you grow accustomed to something or somebody, nothing and no one else can compare! So cry for your first papa. Cry!'

"When she talked like this I regretted marrying under circumstances that put me at a disadvantage, but though I found it unbearable I somehow managed to carry on. I had a little money due me from some people in my native province; so thinking that I might be able to tide over this year end by collecting it, I went all the way back to Ise. But it was no use; I found that my debtors had all left for parts unknown. So I returned this evening just before supper, empty-handed.

"When I entered the house I found that somehow or other my wife had managed to buy firewood and pound rice for rice-cakes. Moreover, the offering tray in front of the Shinto altar had been properly decorated with ferns. The world isn't such a bad place after all, I thought, though there are gods who will abandon you to your fate, other gods will pick you up off the ground. However that may be, I had my wife's good husbandry to thank for all these things prepared in my absence. I felt pleased, and after I called in to my wife that I had arrived safely back home, she seemed more affable than usual. First she brought me water to wash my feet with, and then set before me a supper of sardines, some vinegared and some broiled. Just as I started to eat them, she asked me if I had brought the money from Ise. No sooner did she learn of my failure than she began bawling me out:

"'How dare you come back empty-handed! The rice you are eating was obtained by mortgaging my very person. Unless I pay ninety-five *monme* by the end of the second month I shall be lost. Other people's rice costs only forty *monme*, while ours costs us ninety-five *monme* solely because you are good-for-nothing. You came to this house with no resources other than your single breechcloth, so you'll lose nothing by clearing out right now. It will be dark tonight, so you'd better leave before it's too late.'

"So saying, she took away the tray I had already begun to eat from and urged me to be on my way. Meantime neighbors had come thronging in, and siding with my wife, they said, 'It must be embarrassing to you, but your position as a husband who has married into his wife's household is a weak one. If you are a man at all, you'd better leave this place. You'll probably find a good opportunity for marrying into some other family.' At the time I was too sad even to cry.

Tomorrow I shall return to my native province; but I was so completely at a loss as to where to spend tonight that I came here, even though my denomination is Nichiren."

When his story, at once funny and pitiful, was finished, the last of the three temple visitors laughed aloud and said, "Now it's my turn to tell my story, but please excuse me from telling you who and what I am. I can't stay at home without being tormented by bill collectors, and nobody will lend me even ten *mon*. I felt chilly and wanted a drink, so I hatched up first one crazy scheme and then another, but in the end could think of none that would tide me over the year end. At last I concocted a shameful plan: tonight the story of Heitarō would be told at the temple and crowds of people would come to hear it. While they were listening I would steal their sandals to get drink money. Contrary to my expectations, however, very few people are to be seen tonight in any temple, and so this job, which was to be done under the very eyes of the Buddha, turned out to be impossible, too."

The man shed tears as he told his story. Deeply moved, the priest clapped his hands together and said, "Well, well! Though all of you are endowed with an inherent Buddha nature, it appears that your poverty begets all manner of evil schemes. But such is the sad way of the world."

As he was thus pondering the state of the human realm, in rushed a woman to inform him that his niece had just given birth in an easy delivery. On her heels came a man with a message that the funeral of Kuzō the box maker, who had hanged himself after a quarrel with a bill collector, would be held after midnight. The messenger humbly requested that the priest come out to the cremation ground. In the midst of the ado caused by this good news and bad news, a tailor entered to report that the white kimono that the priest had asked him to make had been stolen when it had been left unguarded for a moment. The tailor promised that if after a search he was unable to recover it, he would reimburse the priest to spare him any possible loss.

Then a man who lived just east of the temple came in to ask the priest to allow him to draw water from the temple well during the first five days of the New Year, because his own well had collapsed. After him came the only son of the most influential member of the priest's congregation, who had spent himself into bankruptcy and found it necessary to leave the city. His mother had gotten the idea of placing him in the care of the priest until the fourth day of the first month. Such a request as this from so rich a parishioner no priest could deny.

So we see that so long as he lives in this floating world, even the proverbially neglected "priest in the twelfth month" is far from being free from involvement in human affairs.

The Perennially
Prosperous Shops of Edo

TODAY PEACE reigns throughout the realm, and
people from all over the land are eager to do business
in Edo. Businesses of every sort open branches there,
and never a day passes but goods from every province are
shipped to wholesalers there by boat or carried on the backs of
thousands of packhorses. No further proof is needed that
there is an abundance of gold and silver in the world, and it
would be a pity indeed if a merchant were unable to figure out
how to lay hands on some of it.

From the twenty-fifth[1] of the twelfth month onward Tōri
Street, with its prosperous establishments, looks like a treasure
mart. The public turns its attention away from shops selling
ordinary things for daily use in favor of those with goods displayed only at the New Year's season: painted battledores from

---

[1] The original gives this date as the fifteenth, but that appears to be a mistake (*SNKBZ* p. 470 note 9; Ihara Saikaku, trans. Teruoka Yasutaka, *Gendaigoyaku Saikaku zenshū*, vol. 11, *Seken mune san'yō, Yorozu no fumi hōgu* [Tokyo: Shōgakukan, 1976] p. 234).

Kyoto and mallets of good fortune, all inlaid with silver and gold, and similar luxuries. Even a miniature bow selling for two *ryō* of gold can find buyers, and these are not only given to the sons of daimyo, for in Edo even the townspeople are extremely generous.

The temporary stalls set up in the middle of the street are doing a brisk business. Copper coins flow like currents of water, while silver piles up like drifting snow. Visible in the distance is Mt. Fuji, rising in all its magnificence against the horizon, while the footsteps of people streaming across Nihon Bridge sound like the rumbling of a hundred million carts. Every morning fish are sold in enormous quantities in the Funa district market, causing some to wonder aloud if the supply in the seas surrounding our fair islands has been exhausted.

Every day to the vegetable market of the Suda district of Kanda tens of thousands of loads of daikon are brought in on the backs of farmhorses, such that it seems as though the very daikon fields themselves were moving into town. So plentiful are the red chili peppers arrayed in tubs there that although in the province of Musashi, one could well imagine oneself to be gazing at the famed autumn colors of Mt. Tatsuta in far-off Yamato. The plethora of wild ducks and geese for sale in the Setamono district and Kōjimachi look like black clouds descended to earth. The kimono fabrics displayed at the shops in Honmachi range from multicolored Kyoto-style dyed cloth to the scattered-pattern cloth worn by the women in samurai households. Taking in this riot of shapes and colors is like viewing the sights of all four seasons at once, and brings to mind the charms of the women these fine materials will adorn. The vast mounds of fluffy silk fiber on display in the shops of the Tenma district recall the snow-clad mountains of Yoshino at dawn. When evening comes, lanterns are hung up in shop fronts, casting their light out into the street. New Year's Eve, the time when merchants make their largest transactions in a single evening, is worth a thousand *ryō* of gold.

As for *tabi* and leather-soled sandals, the artisans of Edo habitually wait to purchase them last of all, just before the New Year begins to dawn. But one year it happened that none were to be found for sale in all of Edo. As might have been anticipated, in the most populous city of Japan the demand was for thousands of pairs of both. Whereas in the early evening the price of a pair of leather-soled sandals was only seven or eight *bu*, after midnight it rose to one *monme* and two or three *bu*, and by dawn it had soared to two and a half *monme*. Even at this price, although there would have been buyers, there were no sellers.

Another year, a couple of dried porgies to be displayed for good luck were priced at eighteen *monme*; still another year, a single decorative bitter orange cost two *bu* of gold. Despite such fancy prices people of Edo did not refrain from buying them. In Kyoto and Osaka, on the other hand, even when an item is needed to celebrate a happy occasion, people are disinclined to buy it if the price is exorbitant. Because of this Edoites are said to have the daimyo spirit. When small-minded people who have lived a long time in Kyoto or Osaka move to Edo, they find themselves so adapting to the ways of Edo that in time they do not even count their coppers or verify the exact weight of their gold coins.

If by mischance a coin of short weight is taken in, it is merely passed along to the next fellow with no further ado. Since money is forever changing hands anyhow, why make a fuss about it?

If one looks into the houses of money couriers, who by about the seventeenth or eighteenth of each month travel to

Kyoto or Osaka, one can see heaps of silver and gold, shining bright as ever. No one can tell how many times a year that money will be travelling back and forth along that same road. There's nothing and nobody in the world that works as hard as money does. Yet even with all this money, there are still people who have to face the coming of the New Year without a single gold coin in hand—even in Edo.

As regards New Year's gifts, the usual items sent by messenger from one samurai household to another include cards describing swords to be presented later, kimono, barrels of saké accompanied by boxed dried fish, and boxes of candles. Each of them gives promise of an endless succession of happy New Years to come. Even the pine decorations before the gate of each home at New Year's symbolize the first stage in the ascent of that Mount of Long Life. And so, as over the Evergreen Bridge[2] the New Year dawns in a calm and cloudless sky, the sun sheds its beneficent beams over all.

---

[2] A direct translation of the name of the Tokiwabashi, a bridge in the Honmachi district of Edo (*SNKBZ* p. 473 note 13.)